THE MAGIC
STRIPTEASE

He grins
Like a clown with a banjo.
He doffs his hat
With happy precision,
Like a flower
Wound up with keys.

R. H. W. Dillard—"Three Friends"

THE MAGIC STRIPTEASE

GEORGE GARRETT

DOUBLEDAY & COMPANY, INC.

GARDEN CITY, NEW YORK

1973

ISBN: 0-385-05034-8
Library of Congress Catalog Card Number 73-79668
Copyright © 1964, 1965, 1973 by George Garrett
All Rights Reserved
Printed in the United States of America
First Edition

All the characters and events in these stories are imaginary.

FOR WILLIAM, GEORGE, AND ALICE

CONTENTS

THE MAGIC STRIPTEASE

A comic strip fable

Gratitude is riches and complaint is poverty
and the worst I ever had was wonderful.

BROTHER DAVE GARDNER

ONE

From Jacob Quirk's Secret Journal

Let us now turn to the old problem of human will power. Let us consider something of the nature of human freedom, the capacity to become.

The limitations of the human will have never been clearly defined. The possibilities of self-control and self-exploitation are mostly unexplored. Barely even suggested or hinted at so far in man's long and longwinded, painful evolution from something more or less like an average tadpole to something more or less like a hairless ape. From nothing and nowhere to where he stands now on two legs on top of the freaking heap. Master of practically everything in the universe. Except, of course, himself . . .

Barely hinted at. And yet the signs and portents, the clues are there. Take, for example, the Indian fakirs [or maybe it's fakers; never was too good at spelling; must re-

member to improve my spelling; look it up in the dictionary (?); or is it dictionery (?)], anyway those wise and
skinny little brown men who can and do lie, all comfortable and cheerful, on top of a bed of tenpenny nails just
like it was a Beautyrest or a Sealy Posturepedic mattress.
Rope climbers! Fire eaters! Sword swallowers! Mystics
standing on one leg, like a crane or something, for hours at
a time. Or upside down, perched on their kinky heads. And
men who stare unblinking into the burning sun, locked in
place like bronze statues, until their very flesh begins to
rot and shred and peel away like old wallpaper and their
eyes cease to see and become nothing but blind, blank
peepholes in the bone.

There are students of karate who can break two-by-fours
and bricks with a swift single blow of the flat edge of the
hand.

But we don't have to be so exotic, do we? I mean, you
can drop in and look around the European Health Spa or
any other local gym or health club. And assuming the fags
in white coats don't bug you into signing up for a lifetime
membership (I knew one guy in the old days so shy and
self-effacing that he signed up for two lifetime member-
ships), you can stand around and observe pure process and
change in action. Men and women sweating and straining,
toting and fetching, lifting and heaving, grunting and
groaning, showering and steaming, all with the singleminded aim of changing the size and shape of their muscles and (sometimes) even the very conformation of their
bones. And they can do it, too, if they keep at it. Look at
the advertisements with "Before" and "After" pictures.
Think of old Charles Atlas. He proved that he could take
a 97-pound weakling and turn him into a muscle-bound

monster. So the next time a bully came around the beach and kicked sand all over him and his girlfriend, he could rise up and kick right back and maybe knock the bully on his ass and then end up kicking him while he lay there, thus giving him something to rise above. That's a lot of crap about your ordinary human being not being able to add a cubit to his stature. (How much is one cubit, anyhow? Don't forget to look it up.) I have heard of people who were able to add an inch, sometimes more, to their height just by hanging in traction for a few hours every day.

See what I mean? See what I am getting at?

Even perfectly ordinary people, just flat faces in the dull crowd, sliding by like sweaty dolls on wheels, just folks, can, have, and do become capable of fantastic feats of strength, self-discipline and imagination if the proper occasion comes along and stimulates the proper glands. They have been known at times of emergency and duress, "in the fell clutch of circumstance," to take and bend iron bars like freshly cooked spaghetti, to run like wild deer in deer season when the sound of the 30/06 is heard in the land (along with the screams and shrill cries of hunters wounding each other). It is recorded that, at times like these, people have played volleyball with huge boulders, have played grabarse with gorillas, butted their heads against charging bulls and rhinos etc.

And don't forget about drugs. All those wild crazy new pills that can get an average human being not only through an average day, but also floating through and above it upon a cozy cloud-9.

Don't forget the wonders of hypnosis.

What I am trying to say is that there is no good reason

5

why anyone in the world should ever have cause to doubt me and my special talent.

Why should they?

Why should I ever have any reason to doubt myself?

TWO

Jacob Quirk, the artist of himself

Jacob Quirk did not come by his unusual (probably unique) skill easily or early. It could not have been a mere genetic gift. Of course he was given certain basic talent. But finally it was, it must have been, a combination of imagination and ruthless self-discipline which, supplementing a natural inclination towards mimicry, made possible the development and ultimate refinement of his art.

He began to imitate other people while he was still a toddler in diapers.

His father, a weary tailor, took a dim view of his infant son's mimetic antics. But his dear mother, a mountainous woman of virtually unquenchable energy and enthusiasm and an incorrigible optimism, she who began each day with a cheerful and obscene greeting to life itself and a half pint of straight gin for breakfast, she encouraged him eagerly. And so very early in life he learned how to amuse her and her many friends (mostly uncles) and at one and the same time to drive bill collectors, door-to-door salesmen, policemen, visiting preachers and teachers, and, of course, his own father to the precipitous edges of raging distraction.

While other little children of his age were playing with their footballs and violins, Jacob was all alone in the basement or the attic making faces at old, gilt-framed, fading mirrors.

One evening he came to the supper table and sat down, wearing an extraordinarily accurate representation of his father's sad, deep-lined, tight-lipped and habitual expression. As he took his place, sat down, pulled up his chair, and lifted his face to greet his parents, his mother took one look at him and exploded into an instantaneous, wild, dissonant braying scherzo of uncontrolled laughter. Whereupon his father ceased carving the meat, carefully wiped his hands and the knife blade on a napkin and then, with the carving knife in his hand and simple murder in his eyes, he began to pursue his laughing wife. Young Jacob watched them, interested, as they ran in a circle around and around him, wondering casually which of them would tire and falter first. And for a while it seemed as if, even though they were indeed tiring, they were sharing the crucial expense of limited energy equally. And thus it seemed most probable that they would slow down gradually and equally like parts of a single windup toy, passing at last into a kind of breathless slow-motion state like a pair of deepsea divers at some enormous depth, vague and deeply green, like lumbering monsters in a dream.

His mother ruined the beauty of this elegant pattern

8

and settled the evidently insoluble difficulty by breaking out of the circle to rush into the kitchen and then immediately return, hefting a half-gallon gin bottle, with which instrument she intended to crown her offending husband. The bottle, however, was an unnecessary precaution. The swinging kitchen door caught his father flush and fair, just as she was re-entering, and knocked him, crosseyed, to his knees. Then, as he knelt there, slumping forward as if into a deep prayer, she dealt him a solid two-handed blow with the gin bottle, a blow the force of which would have driven a circus tent peg into hard ground with one stroke, merely as insurance. This, too, turned out to be wasted effort, an idle gesture; for the poor man was already quite dead, from a savage stroke, before the edge of the kitchen door had struck his jaw. He had felt no pain but the first astounding one.

She knelt down beside him and lifted his battered head into her ample lap. She cried a little. She studied the last sad expression on her husband's face, then frowned and looked up at Jacob. Who was now quietly eating his supper so as not to draw attention to himself. Aware of her scrutiny, Jacob paused, fork in hand, and looked down at her, smiled sweetly, and then made his father's face again.

She laughed so hard she fell on the floor, lying beside her late husband.

"You can call me a walleyed, redassed baboon!" she cried. "But, Jakey, you had it *perfect* that time!"

She opened the still unbroken gin bottle and pleasured herself with a long healthy swallow. Then she looked once more at her husband, and, with a moan worthy of the finest opera diva, she took the carving knife from his hands and plunged it into her heart.

Jacob Quirk was delivered into the hands and care of the State Orphans' Home that very evening. And he was served a second supper when he emphatically denied having touched a bite of his own.

From his father Jacob inherited great patience, a patience that was almost strong enough for the constant vicissitudes of this world. And he acquired a gentle melancholy, a shrewd, keen, skeptical, observing eye, a slight physique, and an ability to live frugally.

From his mother he received an active and sometimes irrepressible sense of humor, a somewhat theatrical temperament, and, of course, an overwhelming, if not insatiable appetite for the good and simple pleasures of this world.

And so it came to pass, ironically, that his mother and his father continued their loving warfare within him, forever circling around and around his astonished but always curious psyche in perpetual frozen motion and rage, she never to break out of the circle by accident or volition, he never to succeed in reaching her with the sharp point or whetted edge of the carving knife, and Jacob forever condemned to be a small boy, trying to mind his own business, anxious to eat his supper before it cools, and doing his level serious best not to be anything except a modest observer, an unpretentious, almost motionless fly on the wall. . . .

Jacob remained in the Orphans' Home until he was legally of age. Other children came and went, were adopted or found foster homes. But no such luck for him. The Director and all the staff encouraged him in his craft of mimicry, but would-be parents found it disconcerting. The more he tried to please, the more he troubled them.

"Nobody likes a smartass kid around the house," the

Director explained to him. "You might as well stay here where you are appreciated."

Later, with the experience of the Orphans' Home behind him, Jacob was able to put his natural abilities to work for himself. After a stint as a clown with a small traveling circus, he became a professional impersonator and a good one, able to create identifiable and funny imitations of public figures, celebrities, and many other noteworthy and notorious people whose expressions, mannerisms, and bad habits were a matter deeply rooted in the mass consciousness, if not, alas, its conscience. He made a good living at this and he traveled far and wide across the land to perform. Perhaps he should have been a happy man. But after the initial pleasure of being able without much effort to evoke the laughter and applause of whole rooms full of intoxicated strangers, he began to feel not altogether satisfied with himself. There was so little challenge. It was all so easy and always becoming easier. There was only the most limited opportunity for his growth and development as an artist. It was, after all, he began to feel, not really an art form at all, but rather a kind of crude demonstration of the craft of caricature. Worse yet, the hollow, scarcely even two-dimensional characters of the celebrities he impersonated, from poets to politicians, from high-class prostitutes to envied public enemies, all those caught for a wink of time in the public's blinking, bloodshot eye, bored him to tears. As for real tears, he could not decide which to weep over (if either were worthy of pity or pathos)—the restless, hopeful, sad-hearted and deceived public which took some pleasure in the reduction of the luckier and more famous into the jangling dimensions of skeletons; or the celebrities themselves, their souls burned

11

away to smoke by too many photographs, clothes and skin peeled away by hostile eyes that swarmed over them, waking or dreaming, like maggots.

Jacob Quirk—whose stage name was now Proteus, the Prince of Impersonators—wearied more and more even as his success led him slowly up the slippery ladder ("Slippery with *what?*" he wrote in his *Journal*. "Better not think about that.") of Success. Inexorably he had moved upward, from sharing the billing and, in plain fact, being a mere interruption between the acts of stripteasers, conventional comedians and crooners, in drafty, lonesome, barnlike, boondocks honky-tonks, to nightclubs, to feature billing, his own name in neon blinking proudly and high on the marquees of famous metropolitan places. He began to appear on stages and on television shows. He was reaching a peak of earning power and in real danger of becoming an imitable celebrity himself.

As an antidote to the slow sweet poison, he began to try various methods of enlarging, enriching, and improving his art form, even as he was earning his living by the practice of it. He soon became a master of a new kind of quick-draw, shot-from-the-hip caricature sketch, a suddenly inspired, spontaneous portrait of random members of his audience.

This was not (needless to report) deeply appreciated. And soon, even though he was refining his skill and a pioneer of new forms of impersonation, it became more and more difficult for him to get work. Evidently the real, live people sitting in the audience of a nightclub or a theater did not feel it was a worthwhile bargain to pay out good money for the privilege of being treated like celebrities and being mocked face to face. Somehow they seemed to consider it as insulting. For some reason, most people assumed that his only purpose was to ridicule them. Faced with a growing unpopularity and not unwilling to make a reasonable compromise, if only for the sake of survival, Quirk turned to the impersonation and re-creation of more general characters, types—people he had noticed on the streets, in parks, on his travels and in the routines of daily life. It made him very happy to be able to do this, and quite soon he had become the acknowledged master of this singular form of impersonation.

Unfortunately, this was not much appreciated either. People, evidently, did not wish to take baths, get all dressed up, go out and pay through the nose just to see ordinary types from daily life being impersonated.

And so the more he developed and polished his art, the less successful he became.

All this was surely bound to lead him towards some kind of turning point or climax. Which event occurred for him in the plush office of his agent at Master Artists' Corp.

"Flush it! Pull the chain on the whole *shtick!*" His agent suggested. "It won't buy us postage stamps."

"Why not?"

"Actually, the naked truth is that it just ain't funny."

"Does everything have to be funny?"

"That is a good question and a deep one. But I couldn't answer it right off the top of my head. I am not too good on cosmic questions and philosophy is not my strongest suit. But this much I will tell you, Jake baby. When you are in this funny business, you are supposed to be, you know, like . . . funny."

"True, but everybody who goes to a carnival or sideshow loves the Funhouse, that wonderful collection of crazy mir-

13

rors where they can see themselves all distorted, fat or thin, tall or short, all twisted out of shape."

"So?"

"You've got to admit that," Jake said.

"So go buy yourself a bunch of crazy mirrors. Build your very own Funhouse. Run around making funny faces. But as far as your act is concerned, Jake, if I may risk simple redundancy, you better flush it down the pipe."

"I can't do that," Quirk said. "I am only at the beginning of something new and wonderful. What it is, I don't know. But I am about to make discoveries. I feel like Christopher Columbus or Thomas Alva Edison. I am on the verge of a major breakthrough."

"And I am on the verge of a major breakdown," his agent replied. "It is impossible to reason with you any more."

"I'm not asking you to reason with me. You're supposed to *represent* me."

"Jake, ole *bambino*, you were without a doubt the best, the very *bleeping* best. No *blank*. You were so funny, man! I should live on ten per cent of the loot you earned."

"You already did," Quirk said, turning on his heel and starting out of the office.

"You'll be sorry!" the agent yelled after him. "You'll be back here begging! A prince? Some prince you are! You are the Prince of Ingrates, the King of Bums! *Listen, dummy, this is a business! Art is for kids . . . !*"

Quite aside from the validity, the relative merits of his agent's professional opinion, Jacob Quirk was through with show business. For the time being, at least. He took such money as he had been able to save during his active career, and he worked out a very careful, strict budget which would most likely allow him to live out his life in peace and obscurity. He retired to a cheap furnished room in an unimportant part of a large city. For a time he did nothing at all, not even thinking. Sometimes he tried to read magazines, but they were all full of the faces of the celebrities he already knew too well. He thought of writing his memoirs, but that was too much trouble, too much like work.

Thus, for a time, his life seemed very much like a perfectly pointless, perfectly relaxed sigh.

Then one day, as he was shaving like any ordinary man, he nicked himself and winced at the sudden brief stab of pain. It was really a fine lathery wince, a very pleasing wince. Smiling slowly, he lowered the razor and, with his face still one-half lather, he began to make some faces again, feeling now again a deep need, more than ever the profound inner stirring, the prompting and call towards some remarkable, perhaps ineffable discovery.

That same day he began to work, almost without ceasing, on extending and expanding the limits of his art. Soon he was probing ever deeper, ever more daring, striving with a total, burning, singleminded fury of concentration to move onward, far beyond the known boundaries of physical, mental, and spiritual impersonation and out into a vague and mysterious realm, as yet undiscovered by other mortals, utterly unknown and unexplored. It was a new and complete involvement.

He began to work towards the goal of total self-transformation.

He read and he studied and he worked. It was gradual. It took much time, enormous patience and persistence, a squandering of all his energy; but at last, with the abrupt and marvelous ease of a little boy who learns he can whistle, Jacob Quirk acquired the ability to change and mold himself (much as a sculptor models soft clay) into any known human shape and form.

Please don't quibble about appearance and reality. What's the use? Which of us will settle that old argument? No, it is quite enough for you to understand that finally Jacob Quirk could, by fantastic exercise of will and skill, transform himself into another human form, a form made of flesh that, like any other similar form, was able to suffer and to rejoice. The pleasure and the pain were real enough, as real as his own.

Even so, he was fully aware of his own identity as Jacob Quirk. It seemed like being in a costume or disguise. This was, of course, a complication and presented certain serious problems for him at the outset, and even more later on. As you will see. But for now, it is enough to understand that, for all practical purposes, Jacob Quirk was able to change himself wholly and to become whatever his imagination, his experiences and his wishes conspired to allow him to create.

THREE

From Quirk's Journal

This new power, which I have at last mastered, gives me great joy. A joy all the more precious, all the more intense because of the long period of austerity, self-denial and abnegation which preceded the achievement.

Even though many good years seem to have been spent, all youth and beauty are now mine for the taking.

At my fingertips are all the possibilities of human experience.

To play upon these possibilities, in harmony or wild dissonance, as upon a keyboard!

No actor, playing a role, trying to create and to become a character, can ever become and know his creation, blood and bone, heart and guts, the pulse and the most fleeting and subtle of sensations, as I can.

No poet or novelist can ever manage to blend himself, to wed himself so completely, into the flux and flow of an imaginary creature's being. I can, if I choose, drown myself in the stream of consciousness of a purely fictional character.

Yet, I must be honest. At least with myself. I've got to admit there are already some minor problems, disappointments even, inherent in my medium of self-expression. For example, my characters, regardless of what or whom I choose to become, are always, by definition, fictional. That is to say, a character created and inhabited by me has no real memory, in fact no past at all save that which I am able to imagine and invent. I am, thus, limited by the limits of my own imagination. Moreover, there will be no future for this character. Once I have left his particular shape and form, he simply vanishes into thin air. He has, therefore, no more life of his own than a suit of clothes on a hanger.

Still, I am (or always try to be) a reasonable man. And the definition of a reasonable man is: he who accepts his limitations. As one accepts one's family and relatives. For what they are. I'm willing to accept the obvious limitations of my art.

Futhermore, it should be noted (let it be noted), that I have achieved this naturally. Without drugs, pills, strong drink, or any of the other aids to a rich, full, illusory life. I did it coldly and rationally. It was done with premeditation.

I intend, insofar as it is possible, to use my acquired talent coldly and rationally. Not for self-aggrandizement. Not for name, fame and/or gain. Not to injure others or exalt myself. Yet only for myself.

I intend to devote myself to my own education, allowing, of course, a modicum of time for simple amusement.

FOUR

Some early anecdotes

At first Jacob Quirk was compelled to work closely, almost photographically from living models, the people he saw all around him in the city. He had advantages. By now he was, even as himself, so anonymous that he passed like a slight, timid shadow in the crowd, always observing, studying everything as cleanly as a camera lens.

At first, indeed, Quirk used a real lens. Not being gifted, hand and eye, to sketch what he saw, he tried the method of the candid photographer. But that was a difficult art too, one which took time, and even though he prided himself (and not without reason) on his patience, he simply did not have time to delay any more. So he tried the more difficult, yet more direct technique of making *himself* a kind of camera, training his memory to record and retain a face, a body, a way of moving, the tilt of a head, etc.

19

One of the first things he decided to be was the postman. He had always wanted to be a postman, from the days at the Orphans' Home, when there was no one to write to him, through the long lonely days in his furnished room. From his high, single, dusty window, how many times he had watched, his face pressed like a moon against the glass or the screen, the postman coming up the sidewalk, shifting the weight of the heavy, mysterious leather bag on his shoulder, bundled against cold or sweating on hot summer days, bearing always in that miraculous grab bag the prizes, the sealed news and secret messages of other worlds. How Quirk envied that burden! The young postman bore a load of pleas, rejections, recriminations, passions and deep desires. He brought bills and ads and the news of birth and death. Love and death lay lightly in his hands.

This transformation was simple and on the whole successful, yet it disturbed him deeply.

How little I know of the people around me, he wrote in his Journal. Who would have dreamed that young Bridges is a drunkard? All this time I thought he was ill or perhaps handicapped by some disease or other.

And take Mrs. Carnassi, the widow Carnassi, whom I have long admired for her impeccable taste, fastidious manners, and her rare (rare in this section of the city) appearance—cool, smiling, and elegant. She has always seemed like the one bright flower of beauty in this crummy neighborhood. And yet, when I was being the postman, she offered herself to me in payment of 8¢ postage due. First said she had the money up in her apartment and would I mind coming up with her to get it. I followed her up the stairs cheerfully. Once inside the door, she turned and told me she didn't have a cent to pay me. And I can believe it. The apartment of the widow Carnassi is bare and empty. No furniture of any kind at all except for one old ripped and stained mattress in the middle of the floor. No objects of any kind. No chairs, no rugs, no curtains, nothing! Except that all the closets are open, bulging and overflowing with clothing. The closets glittering and glowing like open jewel boxes, overbrimming with an abundance of extravagant, beautiful clothes. What a thing! To live like a poor rat. To live almost as poor as poor old Job in order to walk, cool and smiling and elegant, on the streets in fine clothes. And so, even in curiosity and disillusion, I must ask myself—what is the truth about and for Mrs. Carnassi? Is it to strip to the skin hurriedly and then to lie down on a filthy mattress in the middle of the floor, to plead with a young postman to accept the gift of herself in lieu of 8¢ postage due? Why? In the vain hope that the sealed envelope may contain some answer, some shattering marvel of news, some ultimate and undeniable revelation which will change her face and the face of this old world, or at least wipe away the lines of her face and the cruel print of crow's feet at the edges of her bright eyes?

Later, the real postman, coming along his daily route, was somewhat astonished to discover that someone or other, apparently himself, had already delivered the mail in this neighborhood. This was a test for Quirk. Anxiously he watched from the window of his room when the real postman appeared on the scene. He watched him chat amiably with some of the people on the sidewalk, then shrug his shoulders and go on his way briskly, whistling a

21

happy tune, as if what had happened were the most ordinary occurrence in the world. Off went the postman with a shrug and a whistle and not even the burden of suspicion.

So Jacob Quirk concluded that most people most of the time are devoid of the itch of curiosity, that most of them in fact live continually in a senseless, irrational, mysterious and magic world, a universe which even the most remote and isolated of dark-skinned aborigines, clad only in their war paint and loincloths, would find frightening and primitive. Quirk imagined that he could come galloping down the street riding on a noble steed, clad in a suit of armor, St. George out looking for a dragon, and, as long as he didn't run a red light, go up a one-way street in the wrong direction, or begin to tilt and joust with taxicabs and trucks, he would not likely raise a single eyebrow among the crowd of those passing by, so wholly engrossed were they in their own woes and concerns. He decided that people see what they want to see and believe what they care to believe. And this in itself, he ascertained, was at once the strength and the secret of his art.

This knowledge gave him an intoxicating, dizzying sense of his own freedom.

After the first trial run as the postman, he began cautiously to try other adventures, feeling ever more lighthearted, less responsible and less wary. In gradual succession he tried his hand at being the milkman, the garbageman, the laundryman, then even the policeman on the beat. And, of course, from the formal and somewhat abstract viewpoint afforded by these roles, he was able to observe the continually changing, different sides of his neighbors. He learned of their sadness, infidelity, guilt

22

and self-pity. He listened to their pleas, excuses, and out-
bursts of savage temper. He also heard laughter from surprising places, places in which he had previously supposed
the only wine was tears. Often he found himself rudely
abused and mistreated, and sometimes he was extrav-
agantly overrewarded for simple services.

Still essentially a comedian at this stage of his development, Quirk also often indulged himself in harmless
little practical jokes. He was, after all, perfectly equipped
to play the part of a neighborhood Til Eulenspiegel, a poor
man's merry Robin Hood.

Of all the people on the block, the man whom Jacob
pitied most was Agon, the fruit peddlar. Agon reminded
him in many ways of his father, as best as he could remember him. He was old before his time, sad and profoundly
embittered, needing, it seemed, only sackcloth and ashes
and a ruined wall to wail at in order to become a perfect
model of atonement for the sin of having ever drawn his
first breath. Yet tenaciously, clawing with brittle and dirty
fingernails merely to survive, Agon had advanced inexorably forward and upward from a small, rattling pushcart
to his own fruitstand with a faded awning over part of the
sidewalk. Evidently this slow change, this manifest example of what sociologists are wont to call "upward mobil-
ity," was small consolation to Agon.

Thinking about it, Quirk wrote in his *Journal*:

*In our age anything less than the shocking lightning bolt
followed by the thunder rolls (o kettle drums conducted
by Leonard Bernstein!) of Success must be regarded as
Failure. Failure is our great tragedy, our sickness. The failed
are our modern witches, burned daily (metaphorically) in*

23

joyous abandon of the auto-da-fé *throughout the land from coast to coast. Failure is our leprosy. Maybe failures should be required to wear bells like the lepers of the Middle Ages. "All Failures Will Henceforth and Ever After World Without End Wear Bells To Warn Decent Citizens of Their Coming and Going!" A charming idea. But let us assume that it could be enforced. What would happen then? The next morning, following the posting of this notice, bright and early the streets would begin to sing matins. Before noon millions and millions of little bells would be cheerfully ringing. Then the great and the proud, the captains and the kings, suddenly, urgently, and palpably aloof and separate from the rest of mankind, would come forth too, also wearing bells (silver and gold and jeweled ones, to be sure), all protesting a multitude of secret failures in their lives which thus entitled them to rejoin the race. In short, it wouldn't work. But what a swell time to be in the bell business.*

Quirk believed that what Agon, the fruit peddlar, needed above all things was a penny's worth of love or, if that was too much to ask, a few trading stamps redeemable for some slight, occasional signs of affection. Yet, because of his bitterness and his sour, tight-lipped disposition, the very best and most that he could hope for was to die solvent enough to afford a decent band of professional mourners for his funeral. Until then he was condemned to be irascible, choleric, given to violent, vein-pulsing, black-faced, deep-breathing rages against children who stole apples, housewives who poked at and fiddled with his fruit, policemen, tax collectors, the barber next door (a hearty man forever shouting "Beaver!" at the sight of

24

Agon's bushy beard). Agon's only solace was to call down curses upon the heads of them, one and all, in a language most of them could not understand anyway. And so, instead of a small measure of love, he received hatred and ridicule. Not often directly, for he was feared. Mostly they spat on his shadow after he passed by and felt better for doing it.

This is wrong, Quirk thought. He waited for a chance to do something about it.

One day Agon had to leave the neighborhood for a few hours to visit with some relatives, whom he had not seen for many years, on the other side of the city. No doubt it was the funeral of a patriarch or the wedding of a promising youngster which drew him from his familiar arena of anger and shame. No one really knew or cared.

As soon as Agon had safely descended into the subway entrance and disappeared, Jacob Quirk transformed himself and reappeared as Agon. Agon changing his mind. Agon coming back without really going. Agon pulling some kind of a sneaky trick. All this to the intense consternation, the dismay and horror, of the two underpaid and harassed little boys who had been left to watch over the fruitstand. Every inch Agon, Quirk entered quietly, tiptoed into the back and found the boys stuffing themselves with bananas.

"We thought you were gone, Mr. Agon, sir!" they both gulped, simultaneously leaping to their feet.

"I changed my mind," he said quietly. Then with a pleasant smile: "Do you boys like my bananas?"

"We'll pay! We'll pay!" they cried. "We'll work it out in overtime! We promise!"

"Bananas are very good for growing boys. They fill you up and make you fat," he said. "Help yourselves."

The two boys looked at each other in abrupt, startled, doubting profile, like a pair of perfectly matched, Alfred E. Newman bookends. But he seemed to be serious, for he instructed them that today was to be a kind of holiday. He told them to go forth on the block and make the announcement to everyone. Free fruit for everybody! A sort of harvest celebration like the celebrations of the pressing of grapes into wines in certain older countries. An orgy of wonderful fresh fruit: grapes and plums, oranges, and tangerines, bananas and mellons, grapefruit and nectarines and strawberries and apples, and oh, everything good and fine from the rich gardens of this world.

Baffled, still apprehensive and doubtful, they knew at least to do what he told them to. For a few short hours the whole block was itself transformed, becoming briefly a place of joy and singing, a happy island, albeit surrounded by a sea of clenched fists, an ocean of curses. Lips and hands were stained and sticky with sweetness, and the world seemed new again.

When Agon returned from his visit, he was greeted with love and admiration everywhere he turned. Women kissed him and laughingly complained that his beard tickled. Men shook his hand. The children made rhymes about him to insert into their street games. Even the barber embraced him like a general (French) hugging a hero.

Though he never quite understood what had happened during his absence, he managed to restrain his natural suspicion. He took it simply as a sign, perhaps the work of some careless angel who had singled him out, choosing Agon from among countless thousands of others as lonely and sad as himself, to receive the gift of love. And all that was required of him henceforth was to play, as best he could, the smiling and popular role the angel had created for him. He decided that though he might die too poor to afford professional mourners, there was a chance that he would not need them anyway.

Needless to say, Jacob Quirk soon found occasions to serve the cause of secular Justice.

Once, still early in the stages of advancement of his art, he was wandering the streets of the city, away from his own neighborhood, late at night. For his own amusement he had turned himself into a kind of old-fashioned cartoon caricature of a rich man, clothed in contentment, with top hat and cane, big belly and big cigar. He was enjoying himself thoroughly, more or less minding his own business, until a surly young man armed with a sharp knife stepped out of a shadowy alley and attempted to rob him.

"This is a foolish thing," Quirk told him. "Don't do it."

"Why not?"

"I am only pretending to be rich. The truth is that I have very little money."

"I don't give a *blank*," the young robber said. "If you've got a dime, you're better off than I am."

"You'll be sorry," Quirk said. "Crime does not pay very well."

"Oh, shut up, you fat creep!" the young man replied, knocking Quirk flat on the pavement.

All the while he was trying to dissuade the young man from crime, Quirk had been carefully studying him. So, first thing the next morning, Quirk became the spitting image of his midnight assailant and proceeded to rob a large, busy, crowded bank. All of the young man's alibis and explanations, all circumstances of mitigation and extenuation, proved useless after he was arrested by the police and confronted with the unshakable testimony of dozens of eyewitnesses. He was given a fair and speedy trial and then sent off to jail to serve out a long sentence at hard labor.

Quirk never once conceived of this little trick as motivated by a need to revenge the insult of the blow to his head or, indeed, as retribution for the two dollars and forty-five cents he happened to have in his pockets at the time. As he noted in his *Journal:*

I do not ever intend to use my gifts for petty considerations or for personal gain and self-satisfaction. It is perfectly reasonable, on the basis of the evidence, to assume that this young man was bound to end up in jail sooner or later anyway. I have not changed his fate. I have only introduced him to it early, thus allowing him a rare, perhaps invaluable opportunity to know and to come to terms with his eventual manifest destiny. Few men ever are so blessed. And so early in life! At a time when other, less fortunate young men have nothing more to do than to imagine prodigious feats, miraculous adventures, countless conquests, and eternal youth. Someday he may even thank me for it, though I do feel it prudent to deprive him of that opportunity. I have never been able to accept the gift of simple gratitude. It embarrasses me. Now he has three square meals a day and plenty of wholesome labor to keep him from indulging in excessive self-pity. Above all, he has the consolation of knowing that, in the case of the particular crime for which he has been con-

victed and is being punished, he is perfectly innocent, spot-less as a young lamb. This, too, is rare. How many of us can ever enjoy that feeling?

Now Jacob Quirk began to approach life with zest, vim and vigor. It was as if he had been sleeping until now, as if all that had ever happened to him before was only an uneasy dream to be forgotten soon after waking. And, indeed, he woke with excitement each morning (assuming that he had slept in his own form and his own furnished room) to ask himself one question: "What shall I be today?"

He could be one or many. He could enjoy a virtually endless variety or, if he wished, he could content himself with the old, simple pleasures of repetition and recurrence.

FIVE

More from the Journal

Now that I have this form of freedom—and what man known to us has ever had this freedom before, has tasted the wine of freedom and then drunk so deeply?—I must begin seriously to examine the whole pleasure principle.

I think of pleasure because a man in my shoes would be nuts to go out searching for pain.

It is a quite different thing than the possibilities allowed by the limited human imagination. For example, I can easily imagine myself eating Gargantuan meals, drinking rivers, lakes, why not oceans?, of the finest wines and other beverages, enjoying the bodies of vast multitudes of beautiful women, always in the most perfect and idyllic intimacy. But this is not unique. So can everybody else. And everybody else does. There is no real limit to imagined pleasures. Physically, however, lodged in one mortal

31

frame, one housing for the mind and spirit, the human being is much more strictly limited. It is safe to assume, I believe, on the basis of recorded human history and one's own personal experience, that our appetites for pleasures are always in excess of our actual and specific ability to partake of and enjoy them.

However, my particular art, the ability to bring something imagined into a concrete, physical form, a reality, destroys this theorem, upsets the human balance of power. For example, I can (and I will admit to having done so, though only for the sake of pure research) indulge myself in one enormous meal after another by the simple expedient of changing myself from a full and sated form into a lean and hungry one, as often as I choose and as often as need be.

Subjected to scrutiny and reasonable analysis, however, all this seems rather pointless, a waste of both my time and my talent.

I stand firmly for moderation. Moderation in all things. Excess of any kind, even with the unusual prospect of a quick and easy restoration to a state approximating original hunger and innocence and need, tends to dull the senses and to make all pleasures seem tepid.

A man should, of course, always and at all times strive to live keenly, with each of his five senses as alert as possible.

Who would want to live in a lukewarm world? Burning and/or freezing are better.

SIX

Sex life of a prince

Pleasure, then, pure and simple pleasure, together with the Constitutionally guaranteed right to the pursuit of happiness, these were the basic foundations of Jacob Quirk's new philosophy. Basically in the Epicurean tradition (in the best sense, of course). The good, if aging, world offered more pleasure and more variety than he had ever imagined possible while confined within the boundaries of his own form. And you can be sure that he lived avidly and vigorously, that he enjoyed himself to the fullest. In general, though, it must be pointed out (and Quirk would have been quick to admit it if he had been asked) that, at the beginning at least, the almost infinite possibilities of pleasure and the unceasing necessity of exercising the options of choice almost drove him to a lunatic distraction. Put simply, his problem seemed to be

33

as follows: he was forever tormented by the persistently haunting awareness that even while he was pursuing one pleasure and enjoying it fully, he might just as well have been doing something else and enjoying it just as much. At any and all given moments he might as well have been somebody else, somewhere else.

Then, too, there was the complex matter of personal inhibition, of all those fences, restrictions and taboos separating him from forbidden fields and gardens. These were imposed upon him by dint of having been (at least once and once upon a time) a single person named Jacob Quirk, a being with a whole set of tastes and values acquired by the laws of genetics, by the influence of environment and what-have-you; and, as well, being imposed directly upon him from without by the complex fusion of all past history, known and unknown, by present social mores, and by dreams of the future, all those things which the late Dr. Freud so aptly captured and summed up in one splendid word—*superego*.

Free as he was and seemed to be, it seemed he could never be entirely free of all these things, no matter what shape or form he assumed.

Like many others, Jacob Quirk had been lonely throughout much of his life. And he had been especially alone during the long period of time which had been required to achieve the full mastery of his art. While he was still a performing artist in cabarets and nightclubs, he had, of course, taken advantage of the proximity of free-spirited showgirls, prostitutes, groupies and B-girls (and even occasional drunken customers and overly enthusiastic admirers) to relieve himself of his primary animal hungers, thereby enjoying a measure of solace, however temporary and casual

it may, perforce, have been. He had never had an opportunity to marry, and he was, in truth, more than a little
reluctant to take that serious step in view of his own child-
ish experience as a spectator (then and ever after) of the
wedded bliss and tribulations of his parents. Later, during the long period of training and development, he seldom
left his room. Sometimes, though never often and not
with any consistency or regularity, when he lay on his bed,
worn out after a long hard day at the mirror, hoping to
sleep but unable to, he permitted his idle fancy free rein;
and then, inevitably, images of desire danced like sugar-
plums in his feverish brain. At such times, it seems entirely possible that, despite his enormous self-discipline,
self-control and admirable will power, he may have suc-
cumbed to temptation and indulged himself in the abominable bad habit of *bleepblanking* (See Genesis 38:9).
However this could not often have been the case; for
Jacob knew well from the wise old Director of the State
Orphans' Home that such practices would surely stunt
his growth, a truth sadly attested to by the Director himself, who, standing on tiptoes, might have achieved a
height of five feet. And if this were really true, then the
fact that he had (in his own form) long since achieved
full growth was irrelevant. For might not repeated involvement in the paltry pleasure of *bleepblanking* deprive
Quirk of the plasticity which was essential to his art?

It was, therefore, completely understandable, if not
wholly admirable, that Jacob Quirk should have wished to
correct this condition of physical loneliness as soon as possible, especially since it was now within his power to do so.
He had not much enjoyed the time of enforced celibacy,
and it must be remembered by the more fastidious readers

35

that Jacob Quirk had never taken any vow of chastity, and he had expressed no aspirations toward the monastic vocation.

Books, articles and monographs could be written about Quirk's sex research and experiences. Many are already in progress. Until such time as these definitive studies are available and accessible, however, we can sketch in some of the broad outlines.

His new sex life began (as already indicated) on that day when, as the postman, he collected eight cents postage due from the widow Carnassi. When she undressed and, urging him to set down his mailbag and relax and be sociable for a few minutes, making her invitation even more explicit by unzipping his fly and *bleeping* his *blank*, he had no idea that it would lead to anything more than a quick *blop* on the mattress, no doubt in the time-honored "habitual position." However, the widow Carnassi was a most imaginative woman and quickly introduced him to other practices, such as *slurping* and *sifting* etc. In spite of the fact that after it was all over and he had fulfilled his part of the bargain by handing her the letter, she tried to attack him with a pair of scissors, not trying to stab him, but, if possible, to snip off his *blimp*. The letter, it turned out, was merely a bill from a dress shop, cleverly disguised in a plain envelope with no return address, something for which Quirk felt in all fairness he should not be blamed. Nevertheless, he always felt kindly, even warmly, toward Mrs. Carnassi; and, indeed, he returned to that room and that joyous mattress many times in many different forms; always, however, taking precaution that the notorious scissors were nowhere in sight.

Soon, as his self-confidence increased and along with it

his store of knowledge derived from practical experience, only the universal limitations of time and space could confine him.

Needless to say, all his conquests were easy, since he had every conceivable example of the human form and face at his service.

Conscience and inhibition prevented him at first, indeed *forbade* him, from actively enjoying the entire range of human sexual experience. For example, it seemed decent and manly enough to transform himself into a woman if his sole purpose were to gain access to places and areas which are usually forbidden to men—ladies rooms, baths, solaria, dressing and fitting rooms and so forth. This had the value of pure research and, research or not, would have to be classified as an innocent, perhaps even amusing, diversion. But he simply could not take upon himself the other half of the conventional sexual experience. After all, would that not be morbid curiosity? Might it not be called a kind of homosexuality? And if the latter were so, then did not the very wish or notion of becoming both the giver and the taker betray that unspeakable tendency as much as any overt act?

Jacob Quirk wrestled with this dilemma. He tried to settle it for himself reasonably, by debate and argument. In an early entry he wrote:

If I were indeed a physical woman at the miraculous shuddering moment of mutual surrender and intimacy, then what? What the hell difference does it make if at that same moment I am still acutely conscious of being none other than Jacob Quirk? I mean, if I go as far as clothing myself in the body of a woman, it's a damn sight better

37

and different than those guys who go around "in drag."
Anyhow the cops will bust you for that if they catch you.
They're right too! Too many fags and transvestites run-
ning around the city already. Corrupting the youth. Tak-
ing husbands away from wives, fathers away from families.
Probably Communists trying to sap and drain moral fiber
of nation!

For a short period, he felt it his bounden duty to attack this moral evil at the root. He failed, of course, but it served for a time to give purpose and direction to his activities. And many the horny faggot who was scared *bleepless,* as the saying goes, to find one who had seemed a willing partner suddenly transformed into a square-jawed, blue-eyed, archetypal example of an outraged plainclothes detective from the Vice Squad.

But aren't there many, if not most, men who have at one
time or another dreamed of being women and vice versa?
Quirk wrote. *And, anyhow, according to the majority of*
the best available sources, aren't all human beings indis-
criminately composed of a little of both?

It is a painful experience to read the entries of Quirk in his *Journal* at this point, observing him as he wavers between resolve and rationalization, admiring his strength of character enough to feel some sense of shame, even embarrassment, as resolve weakens and rationalization takes the upper hand. To some, even among the most liberal-minded, it may well seem the first move, however slight, toward a life of debauchery and depravity, just as, to the sensitive intelligence of the true grammarian, the first careless omission of a comma between two independent clauses connected by a co-ordinate conjunction can be and, indeed, has been called "the first step toward utter abandon."

Look at it this way (we find Quirk writing). What I have already accomplished, all that I have already done, only serves to add more evidence to the already widely accepted hypothesis that we can never really and truly know each other. Words are gibberish! Gestures are gobbledygook! The only way we can even come close to knowing each other is carnally. Carnal knowledge! Something they are ready to bust you for too. If you don't ask permission first. (Always remember to ask permission.) Carnal knowledge the only true communication. Yet even at peak of ecstasy and self-abandon, isn't the soul (self, if you insist) able and even likely to be absent and elsewhere? The whore in cheap hotel room consoles herself, even as faceless, nameless lovers labor and strain (hard labor ha! ha!) over her body, that she, the real she, is not there at all but really and truly and always a little girl in a spotless new white dress going to First Communion.

Yet, in the end, it is resolve that wins, after all. Firm resolve, purpose and, if you will, a certain noble dedication, all these shine forth in the scribbled words of Quirk's *Journal*.

I conclude it would be a betrayal of the nature of my gift if I deliberately excluded any human experience just because of my pride or scruples.

I shall not betray humanity. Shall not betray my own human nature.

All humanity is the raw material of my art.

I serve all humanity. I celebrate all things human. But how, unless I have knowledge?

How to know the nature of refinement without being aware of coarseness? How to be a connoisseur without first having tasted all, even the bitterest leavings and dregs?

It is my duty to try everything at least once.

"Duty is the sublimest word in the English language." (R. E. Lee)

"Let copulation thrive!" (William Shakespeare. Polonius' speech to Laertes?? Or was it Falstaff?? Othello?? Romeo??)

Thus, with grit and determination, Jacob Quirk accepted the very grave responsibility, the burden of his art. He went forth and became man and woman, lover and beloved. From his hurried notes, for he had less and less time during this intense and difficult period for his *Journal*, it is clear that he could have written an almost definitive study. He could have topped Krafft-Ebing. He could have made Dr. Kinsey look like a cub scout. He could have made Theodor Reik read like Emily Post! Ovid like *Ideal Marriage!* Boccaccio like Ralph Waldo Emerson! Andreas Cappelanus like Norman Vincent Peale! Henry Miller like Henry James! Norman O. Brown like Louisa May Alcott! Masters and Johnson like Nordhoff and Hall! Petronius like Podhoretz!

But, alas, except for a few notes and one or two interesting episodes and anecdotes, he devoted himself so completely to his research and scholarship, that he has left for posterity very little in the way of specific, documented information.

Not that he didn't grin and bear it. Not that he didn't enjoy himself. In truth, there is some indication that, adhering to his initial pleasure principle, once he had shed the last veils and fig leaves of conformity, he rollicked and rioted like a colt in clover as he explored the whole realm of sexual experience.

Throughout all his interesting experiences and unusual adventures, however, he was not without trouble and anxiety. Evidently he found and deeply regretted the fact that he was never able to establish a perfect, naked rapport with any other human being. There is evidence that there were terrible, heartbreaking times, when, locked in the embrace of some beautiful or exceptional lover, he longed to reveal the truth about himself. He wanted to cry out in confession: "I am not who you think I am. I am only Jacob Quirk, poor Prince of Impersonators, in disguise as usual. I can prove it to you. Give me half a chance!"

But, of course, for a tedious multitude of mundane reasons, this was impossible. The power or revelation was at his fingertips, yet he could not use it. So gradually Quirk became more and more bitter. All his conquests were, in the last analysis, empty. No one could love him for himself alone. Though from his view, which, after all, was much like that of any lover, it seemed little enough to ask, it was far too much to be granted.

SEVEN

From the Journal

Who the hell am I anyhow?
Who do I think I am?
Nobody?
Nobody!
I AM NOBODY!
   That's exactly who I am. Nobody at all save for what-
ever shape and form, whatever shell of flesh and bone, I
happen to be living in (hiding in?) at any given moment.
   I always used to think of my art as putting on. *Putting*
on a disguise. Putting on makeup. Putting on a costume.
Like acting. Now I must admit it is all really taking off.
Hide and seek where I hunt for myself. A hopeless treas-
ure hunt! What would have happened if Cinderella's
slipper fit the Prince? Call it all a magic striptease. Narcis-
sism raised to the nth power!

All I have ever been looking for in a thousand guises and disguises is myself.

Too much time looking in mirrors.

Self-copulation like the worms (I forget which worms) in Biology 101.

Am I a worm?

Ha! Ha! Ha! What a joke!

When I was nobody all the time.

God save me!

Whip me, furies! Whip me, honest knaves!

I hate myself.

EIGHT

An anecdote from the Journal

MEA CULPA
By Jacob Quirk

Sometimes I think I am turning into a monster. The other evening, for example, not being able to think of anything better to do, I transformed myself into a handsome, golden-haired youth. I used Michelangelo's David for my basic model, proportion, conformation of bone and muscle etc. I have found this model to be a rather acceptable one to both sexes. I must confess, however, that I envy Michelangelo. How lucky he was to be able to work in stone!

Dressed in fine, beautifully tailored evening clothes, I sallied forth to attend a fashionable opening at the Opera. Like most people, I despise opera as an art, or, to be honest and even worse, I am utterly indifferent to it. But in the world we live in, it is one of the few places where I can feel really at home when I am being beautiful and all dressed

45

up; at ease there, among the phony gilt and ostentatious mirrors, the plush opulence of a silly, bygone time, replete with the odor of nostalgia, moving among others who, if not always beautiful, are anyway decorous and splendidly attired.

Quick as I got there and made an easy entrance into the lobby, I began to look about for "game," settling, at least for the time being, on a strikingly beautiful young woman. I saw her briefly in the lobby and then later seated in a box behind and above me. She was wearing marvelous jewels and furs. She was cool, elegant, poised, possessing a flawless complexion and an evident state of superb bodily health, the kind which only continuous and very expensive care can maintain.

I recall now that, looking at her as an artist, I tried to keep her form in mind, wanting to try it out myself some-day. It would be like being made out of silk, I suppose. From sow's ear to pure silk! She was truly a wonder of beauty. At the sight of her I caught my breath. My heart seemed to surge, and my loins twitched and shivered for sure.

Let's face it, Jake. She was the kind of broad who wouldn't spit on the real you if you were dying of thirst. She wouldn't bliss on you if you were on fire. She wouldn't touch your dingdong if it was hanging on a Xmas tree.

There was an older man (an old blart about my real age) sitting beside her in the box. Fat and balding, dyspeptic too, judging by the way he pursed his lips as if to fight against an irresistible urge to belch. Sleepy too. Certainly bored silly with being at the Opera. I couldn't blame him. It wasn't even good enough to put a man to

46

sleep, and it turned out to be much too loud to let you sleep even if you were already so inclined and able.

Maybe he was her husband. In any case, there was no doubt that he was the dutiful provider of those furs and jewels, of her hairdressers and massages, of her perfumes and gowns and shoes and everything else, visible and invisible.

I pitied the poor old fool. There he sat, unhappily having to live in one constant flesh, a body that was aging and uncomfortable, already wearing out, already decaying. So if he wanted beauty in his life, he had to purchase it, and even having done so, having paid the price, he could only wear it like a decoration or a flower. Except for my art, I might easily have been in his shoes. If I could have afforded his shoes.

Still, even feeling sorry for him, I had no intention of letting my natural sentimentality interfere with my plans for the evening.

Just before the lights dimmed and the overture began, I managed to attract her attention. For some time she had been slowly, imperiously surveying the audience below her through a pretty pair of opera glasses. They moved methodically up and down rows, her lips in a slight pout, as if all that she saw disgusted her. Then they came to a stop, rested on me, and she reacted visibly. (After all, I was rather special that evening.) She lowered her glasses, and in that brief instant before the last lights faded and the dreadful sounds from the orchestra pit soared upward and filled the huge room, we exchanged swift, urgent messages without a word or gesture, using only the invitations and innuendos of our locked eyes.

At the intermission she approached me, looking per-

fectly at home in the ornate lobby, the lobby in fact look-ing better, somehow more plausible and fine because of her radiant presence there. She used the ancient and honor-able pretext of asking me for a light. As I lit her cigarette for her, she opened a small, thin, gold cigarette case and offered me one. There was a folded note inside which I promptly and discreetly palmed.

Then she had the feverish audacity to take me by the arm and lead me over to meet the old blart she was with. She introduced me as a friend of a friend, and a real Italian count.

"I never saw a blond wop before," he said, eyeing me suspiciously.

"In the North," she said quickly.

Her voice was rich and dark like good brandy, yet some-how lively too, like the very best champagne.

"Yes," I said. "Do not forget the influence of the Nordic barbarians."

"I thought you looked more like a Kraut," he said.

We continued in this fashion, discussing such nonsensi-cal topics as the fate of the blond in the emerging tide of Third World color, the possible results of worldwide mis-cegenation, which, he assured me, was the sole aim and purpose of the U.N. And from there, ironically, he made a dexterous logical leap worthy of Pascal or Kirkegaard, to the pleasures of poontang. Our race might disappear, but by God, there would be good sport for all of us during the age of mongrelization. Then after that we would all get together and exterminate the Jews, who had started the whole thing anyway. Or else we would crossbreed them with Eskimos, and wouldn't that be something? They like

48

furs anyway. Imagine an igloo pawnshop not far from the North Pole!

He finally smiled at me, showing a very fine set of false teeth, when I was able to agree with him wholeheartedly and without reservation that opera was a no-good, bastard art.

Then the lights blinked and the little bell rang. I bowed a nice European good-bye and returned to my place. Just as the lights began to fade again, I managed to read her note: "I shall develop a dreadful migraine headache during the second intermission. Do not return to your seat. Meet me outside near the box office. I shall be alone. Written in the dark and with haste, but with deep feeling by one whose overwhelming desire is to be, however briefly it must be, yours etc."

As soon (and it was a hell of a long time too) as the curtain came creaking down again and the lights went on, I scooted outside the building. I found a drunken bum, gave him my ticket and arranged for an envelope containing five dollars to be held for him at the box office if he would consent to sit in my seat throughout the third act. Then I waited. It was a cold night and a fine light drizzling rain was falling on the city. Occasional taxis, looking like slow, fat tropical fish, floated by, hunting for fares.

Near me I noticed a legless beggar squatting on some kind of homemade wheeled contraption and huddling close to the building for protection against the weather. I fished in my pocket and found a coin for him.

A few minutes later, she came running lightfooted out of the building, glancing over her shoulder with apprehension as though she expected to be followed.

49

"Quick!" she cried. "The sonofablip suspects everything!"

I knew that this must be true. Yet I could hardly enjoy her little game of alarm and pursuit as a prelude to lechery. Suspect or not, we would not be followed. In my mind's eye I could see him and I could feel what it would be like to be sitting up there now sadly alone in the box, the tight, starched shirt collar digging into the folds of his neck, his vast soft belly sagging beyond hope of repair, a slow, steady crawling of sweat along the gross body concealed within his expensive evening clothes. I knew and pitied him. I remembered, for some reason, that my mother had been a fat woman too. But I knew, too, that occasionally even nature offers a small measure of mercy. He would soon be snoring contentedly while the violins scurried to keep up with the soprano and the woodwinds washed their hands of the matter.

We passed by the beggar on wheels. He raised his soft cap to me, winked and smiled a gap-toothed smile. She shivered and, drawing her fur more tightly about her, clung to me, head high.

"I can't abide that," she said a little later.

"What?"

"Ugliness, deformity, suffering . . . I only want to look at beautiful things."

"That must be because you are so beautiful," I said.

"No!" she protested. "I'm not. I'm ugly, full of ugliness inside where it doesn't show. But I can see that you are truly beautiful inside and out."

"Do you really think so?"

"I must be out of my mind. Here I am risking everything just to be with you."

50

"Everything?"

"Well," she said, giggling, "let's just say my present situation."

And so began a long night together, a night made up, it seemed, like a patchwork quilt, of all the lonely, furtive, guilty dreams and wishes of puberty, recalled from wherever it is that dreams go, somehow reunited, joined together, bodied forth, given flesh, our flesh, the flesh of two beautiful bodies, set to dancing like an elaborate kind of windup toy fit to beguile and amuse a bored oriental prince. The extent and nature of her lust staggered even my imagination.

"Beautiful people are a law unto themselves," she told me.

I was also astonished at my own involvement, the curious manner in which, knowing full well I was merely an actor playing a role, I nevertheless played my part so well as to give her a sense of complete satisfaction.

At last, with the night dying, the last few stars fading, and already the faint inextinguishable sounds and murmurs of dawn announcing the coming of a new day to the city, she fell into a deep sleep in my arms. I lay there awake, cradling her gently, alone with my thoughts.

Now I felt an enormous, irrational compassion for the poor man left at the Opera. Tears welling in my eyes, I pictured him coming home someplace, alone, undressing, padding heavily into the bathroom, leaving his teeth to soak in a glass for the night, and finally falling asleep in a wide bed, on his back awhile, breathing asthmatically, then snorting, rolling over to be pillowed by his huge tub of guts. A great stranded whale, dying on the beach. While through his head danced all the commonplace nightmares

51

of our times. In the fever and frenzy of her excitement, gritting and grinding her pretty teeth, she had described him in gross, ugly detail, leaving nothing unsaid, exposing him pitilessly and as completely as she could to me—a perfect stranger. And at that moment, this vicious monologue had only served to whet my own appetite. To my shame. It was as if he were present, as if he were being made by force, against his will, to be witness to the whole episode. Perhaps in his mind's eye he was such a witness. . . .

Then I thought of the beggar in front of the Opera. If only truth could be made known, be shown undisguised in this world, then no doubt but his stumps were far more beautiful than all her healthy, perfumed, hungry parts.

I began to hate myself for allowing myself to be part and parcel of her dreams and delusions. It is a terrible thing to realize that whatever one is, in any shape or form, one is only a character in someone else's dream. It is worse, far more unnerving than those cold, breathless moments when one is trapped in the horror of one's own dream and unable to wake up, to escape from the dream. In another's dream one is captured and enslaved for as long as the alien dream may last.

I determined to pull a little trick on her, something which might teach her a lesson. I had done just such a thing once before under different circumstances. My companion on that occasion was a singularly haughty southern girl, who availed herself of all the old cliches of her tribe, a superb example of dainty, helpless, ineffectual, holier-than-thou, antebellum ladyhood. As soon as she dozed off, I transformed myself into a huge, hulking Negro, black as a clarinet or a coal scuttle. When she yawned and awakened, I waited for her reaction of shock and horror. In-

stead, she lay back on the pillow and shook with laughter.

"See what happens when I don't wear my contacts?" she said. "Can't see a freaking thing without them. Come here, boy . . . !"

She made love to me more avidly than before, crying out a string of four-letter words as if they were a succession of little prayers, a kind of profane rosary.

This time I wanted something more than irony. First I considered the idea of returning to my original, natural form; but it was likely that such a course would expose me to ridicule. I discarded the idea at once.

Sometimes I think that the fear of being ridiculous is the most profound, most urgent emotion of civilized man. It is this fear which goads us into incredible vices. It is this fear which seems to bar us from virtue as effectively as the angels with flaming swords forbid entrance at the gates of Eden.

Next I thought of becoming her companion at the Opera. Now, that should, indeed, have been a shock to the young lady; but it was probably one which she was able, if not prepared, to cope with. Besides, that might subject him to the cruel spotlight of more ridicule. I toyed next with the notion of becoming, for her edification, the very model of a loathsome old man: foul breath, rheumy eyes, a stinking, wrinkled, shriveled horror, made of flesh like a dried fig. That would certainly make her bug her pretty eyes and give her something to think about. My concept was worthy of the best surrealist painters. And, ah!, my toothless, red-gummed smile would be a drooling master-piece!

Then, as I chuckled to myself imagining the scene, a

53

wild, pure, sudden inspiration swept through me. Of course!

With an incredible effort of will, taxing my talent to its farthest limits, I was able to become the very image of the legless beggar at the Opera.

Then I waited.

When at last she began to wake up, groaning a little, stretching like a contented cat by a fire, and reaching for me tenderly, yet eagerly, her eyes still closed, her lips forming a slow, sensual smile, I took her tightly in my arms. Her long eyelashes fluttered and she opened her eyes. I tipped my soft cap, winked and smiled just as he had. She opened her mouth to scream but no sound came. She turned as pale as piano keys and a cold sweat bathed her whole body. And her eyes—wide, shocked, staring at me in hypnotized, unblinking horror—her eyes were the most wounded things I had ever seen.

She found her breath and the screaming began, so I vaulted off the bed and scuttled across the floor, cackling like a madman.

Since then I have made careful and oblique inquiries about her. I hear that she is quite mad. She tried, and not without some success, to disfigure herself. I understand that she has to be kept under what is euphemistically referred to as restraint, strictly confined in what is no longer called a madhouse.

I only wanted her to know the truth.

Dear God, I have sinned.

I didn't mean to hurt her.

Forgive me.

I have never meant to do harm to anyone.

NINE

Prince and pauper

Jacob Quirk was all too human. In spite of the unusual talent he possessed, which raised him above the average, he was beset by all of humanity's nagging swarm of guilts, anxieties, doubts and fears. Added to this was a very real sense of remorse for some of the things he had done himself and done to others. For example, the lady at the Opera.

Like everyone else, he could live cheerfully with all this most of the time, but at other times it drove him to the sheer edge of madness, from which perilous site he peered down into the elemental abyss.

Being supremely rational, he decided to do something about this situation. Obviously to remain the passive victim, repeatedly assaulted and ravaged by guilt and remorse, was a foolish, engraved invitation to lunacy. The thing to do was to atone. But how could he atone?

He had not yet accumulated any great number of possessions to sell or give to the poor. And clearly everything he had or ever would have could not make the least scratch or dent in the castiron condition of poverty in this world. He had, in fact, nothing at all worthy of sacrificing except his art itself. He toyed with the idea and concluded that simply to renounce his art would not be satisfactory. It would not be a significant gesture. Gradually he reached the painful conclusion that he must *use* his art in the service of atonement. He managed quite easily to justify this plan with his principle of pleasure; for though there might be extremely unpleasant, even painful moments, these would add up to a sum of immeasurable pleasure and freedom. It was the teleology of the thing which mattered.

He went at his penance with zeal and gusto. He cheerfully took on all forms and shapes of human suffering. He became grotesquely crippled. He made himself maimed, mutilated, ugly, and loathsome beyond description. He was fully aware that there was something slightly false about all this, that it was a little like a rich boy playing at being poor, knowing that a postcard, a collect telephone call, a telegram can at any time bring him succor. He even considered finding some singularly suffering and repulsive form and vowing to inhabit it for the rest of his life. However, would this be enough? Would it not be even more penitential to use all his power to suffer as much, in every possible way, again and again? He embraced suffering eagerly. He took pain and humiliation to him like a pair of lovers.

None of this proved completely satisfactory. As he wrote:

I have been hoping for pity and compassion, if not for love. Has this hope, this wild desire, corrupted the whole purpose of my penance? Who knows? All I know now is that pity, rendered truly and freely, is as rare as love. Both are as rare as a pair of unicorns. Perhaps both are extinct. Have we evolved beyond such crude states of feeling? (Subject for a monograph some day?) In truth, pity and compassion must be much like love. And, alas, just as in love, the pity to be gained by artifice and illusion is without meaning. But can love or pity ever be earned at all without tricks and sleights of hand? Who knows? No! Who cares?

Still, the experience of suffering and degradation *per se* was not entirely meaningless to Quirk. Even though he was soon aware that neither atonement nor compassion was possible for him (or perhaps for anyone else), he was able to learn something and to profit in another way than he had intended. Never before had he imagined that there were so many rich varieties of human suffering. They far exceeded all the possibilities and subtleties of pleasure. And even though he had failed to arouse much interest in other human beings, no matter what pitiful shapes he assumed, he was able to interest himself.

At last! he wrote in a bold and joyous *finis* to the whole affair. *At last I am able to live with myself without shame. I know that I need not be ashamed of myself ever again!*

From this he learned to pity other humans, those who were unaware of this simple truth. At first, like his father, the patient and unsuccessful tailor, he had longed for the simple grace and dignity of sackcloth and ashes. He imagined a great wall, oh bigger and larger than the Great

57

Wall of China, at which he and all of mankind might someday be permitted to kneel and wail.

Then he had remembered his loving mother, who could pause to laugh while kneeling beside the corpse of her husband.

Which was the true image of humanity?

Wrestling with himself, he gradually began to realize that he had somehow been chosen, that his gift was indeed a gift, something awarded to him among all men, quite as much as if a real and shining angel had appeared before him and said, "Hail, Jacob, full of grace etc." If he had been chosen, then why? For the same reason, no doubt, which others—Samson, Job, Joseph, Judith, even old father Abraham—had been chosen for some special blessing and plan. All that remained was to isolate precisely what his gift implied and what, as a result of all his experiences, he could tell to other creatures which they did not already know, or, if they knew, did not pause to consider as they went on their weary way.

That was it! He must go forth and teach. He must tell them what he had learned.

TEN

More from the Journal

Now I am ready to go forth and to tell them all. Tell the lucky ones, not just the healthy and wealthy, the hale and hearty, the beautiful and the successful, but all who are alive and therefore . . . lucky. Tell them what? Tell them to free themselves from foolish fears. From illusions and self-delusion. From useless sorrow and anguish. To tell them that the only thing worth doing, in the brief wink of light that we call a lifetime, is to learn again and again to suffer and to rejoice.

It is all so simple. I simply shrug my shoulders and a great weight, like an invisible yoke, is lifted off.

What a noble gesture is the shrug! Man alone, unique in the animal kingdom, can shrug when he feels like it. How eloquent! Logic plus eloquence equal rhetoric. I must teach the rhetoric of the shrug.

59

But now that I have the answer, *how* can I tell them? How can I most effectively and efficiently give to the world the benefit of all my experience and hard-earned knowledge?

Suppose, just for the sake of argument, I choose to appear in some altogether beautiful form, all dazzling and joyous and shining. The perfected example in the flesh of all that I have to say. Then what? Experience teaches me I will only become an object and an occasion for envy. Even at best, only a cause and source of desire instead of inspiration.

If, on the other hand, I choose some meek and abject form, something ordinary or ugly. The very picture of the worst the world can do. Then what? Suppose, for example, in the form of a twisted, drooling spastic, I stand before them and moan hallelujahs in praise of Creation? The best I can hope for is to inspire fear and shame. Which are the father and mother of rage.

What if I come as a hero? Alexander the Great or perhaps some movie star? Everybody knows that heroes are mere shabby figments of the collective popular imagination. Nobody will believe a word I say.

As myself. Just plain Jacob Quirk. Would anyone listen? If anyone listened, who would believe?

Suppose I demonstrate my gift? Show off the marvels of my art to the multitude? Experience tells me, even though they will be for a time amused, at least until the novelty wears off, they will proceed at once to misinterpret everything. The thing in itself, the *ding in the dong,* is what will interest them. The worst will want to be entertained. The best will prefer to categorize the experience, labeling it as mere miracle or magic. Then when I try to preach my Message, they will hoot and jeer and boo and hiss.

"Who do you think you are, anyway?" they will demand.

And then I shall have to tell them the truth.

"Nobody."

ELEVEN

An episode in the park

It was a fine spring day. In the public park birds whistled and sang, hidden among fresh new leaves. Flowers bloomed brightly in pretty little plots. The signs—NO SPITTING, KEEP OFF THE GRASS, DON'T FEED SQUIRRELS, FOLKSINGING FORBIDDEN etc.— were all newly painted. So were the fences and railings. Young lovers strolled hand in hand, talking in whispers together. Children ran and played, swift and shrill, cheerfully ignoring all the rules and signs. Maids and mothers slouched along behind baby carriages. Somewhere a carrousel was turning to a lively tune. Ice cream was being sold. A balloon man moved majestically through the park, solemnly holding aloft his bouquet of joy. On benches old men played chess and checkers or snoozed and dreamed in an April daze.

Officer Clancy A. Murdock, an aging policeman assigned to patrol this peaceful park (a mild punishment, really, for this public servant who had, as some urban cops are wont to do, accepted one gratuity too many from concerned criminal types as well as overlooking some modest midnight burglaries performed by his brother-in-law), waddled along the path enjoying every moment of this beautiful day. His collar was loose. His visored cap was cocked at a jaunty angle. His nightstick might as well have been made out of sweet licorice. It felt as light as a conductor's baton or a magician's wand. Officer Murdock pinched and patted a few fannies of maids, winked at some of the growing girls. Once he even stopped to buy some bubble gum for a ragged ratpack of little boys.

Oh, it was a perfect day. Once in a *bleeping* million.

Even though Officer Murdock could not carry any tune for long, he was whistling something or other as he rounded a quiet curve in the path and came face to face with an incredible apparition, the first sight of which shattered his mood of serene tranquility, cut off his whistling in midnote, flushed his psyche of illusions as thoroughly as any Aristotelian tragedy, and made his large, weary feet begin to ache again with the pains of all his years.

"Jesus Christ!" Officer Murdock exclaimed.

A man (he guessed it must be male) was coming, skipping and bounding along the path, directly towards him. Long-haired and bearded, clad in a long, loose, seamless garment that seemed rather like an old mattress cover or a burlap *mumu*. Also hippie sandals. He appeared to have strongly Semitic features and, in spite of the grotesquely bright smile, sad and vaguely familiar eyes. The man was carrying a large homemade sign—poster paper nailed onto

64

something like a bed slat—upon which was crudely printed a single word: REJOICE!

"Just what in the hell are you supposed to be?" Officer Murdock inquired.

"You guessed it the first time," the man told him. "Here I am, laughing and scratching, and all ready to preach to the people."

"You even got the sign wrong, you dummy," Murdock explained. "It's supposed to say *Repent!*"

"No mistake. I painted it all by myself."

"What are you—some kind of a nut?"

The man did not answer at first. He only smiled. He smiled, all sweet and forgiving, at Officer Murdock.

Unfortunately, if there was one thing that deeply outraged Clancy A. Murdock, it was a patronizing lunatic.

"That's a matter of opinion," the loony began to tell him. "The very best modern psychiatrists agree that being nuts is a relative thing."

But Murdock had already grabbed him tightly by his beard and with the aid of his nightstick, applied to the *solar plexus*, was urging him off the open pathway and into the camouflaged seclusion of some shrubbery.

"You listen here," Murdock said. "I don't know what in the *bleeping blank* you are up to, but whatever it may be, I most strongly urge you to cease and desist before I am forced to bust you."

"But I don't plan to break any laws or ordinances."

Utterly blasé. Obviously ruthless, cold and calculating. A guy with all the angles. The man continued smiling sweetly at him.

Officer Murdock was boiling with fury, but he managed to control his feelings admirably.

"Look, is this some kind of a publicity stunt?"

"Not really."

"Are you trying to sell something?"

"Only an idea."

"How much does it cost?"

Cleverly, Officer Murdock tried to trap this criminal into a premature admission of intent to commit a misdemeanor, if not a felony.

"It's for free."

"Who are you working for?"

"I work for God," the man had the unmitigated gall to answer.

Murdock removed his blue, badged, visor cap and mopped his bald head with a handkerchief.

What was the world coming to? Everybody—and not just niggers and Jews and juvenile delinquents—the whole *barfing* bunch has gone ape. No denying that. Even the most basic distinctions between good and bad are being blurred. The way things are going, before long a sane man can't even take sides any more. All he can do is shrug and turn away. It's time to give it all back to the Indians. If you can find any Indians left who want it. . . . Must be the fallout, he figured. They keep blowing up them bombs. And they may even get to me, *me* with the constitution of a pack mule and the sanity of any I.B.M. machine.

Thinking of this distressing predicament and the condition of modern man, Officer Murdock almost felt a little sorry for this foolish man.

"I don't think you know what you're doing," he volunteered. "Do you know?"

"I have never been so sure of anything in my entire life."

"Take a word of advice from an oldtime flatfoot, a long-time member in good standing of the benevolent fraternity of the fuzz. I have been around for a long time, and during that time I have seen a thing or two."

"I do not doubt it."

"Believe me, people, and especially members of the true faith, and most especially those who, like myself, are tied by heritage and tradition to the apron strings of Mother Church, believe me, folks just don't take a kindly, objective, nonviolent view of other folks who get all dressed up and pretend that they are Our Lord. I don't care what the Supreme Court says. I don't care if the Chief Justice himself comes into the Supreme Courthouse and presides in a getup like yours, people are not going to think it's funny. Religion being what even you will have to agree is a sensitive subject, it don't amuse them a whole hell of a lot."

"Thank you for your eloquent and gratuitous counsel," the man said. "But I want you to understand that I am not pretending to be anything."

"Oh," said Officer Murdock, suddenly all sly again. "Then I suppose you really are Jesus Christ."

"Nope," the man said. "My name is Jacob Quirk, and I am the Prince of Impersonators."

"For heaven's sake, man! Pick somebody else to impersonate."

Eventually, after much discussion, some of it frankly heated, Officer Murdock had to admit that he was required by law to release Quirk's beard and to let him go his way in peace. Nevertheless, Murdock followed along behind him, hidden, concealed, but close enough so that midway in Quirk's speech to the crowd, just when the riot was really getting started good, he was able to come crashing out of the bushes to the rescue, blowing his police whistle like a drunken, old-country banshee, and with some difficulty deliver Quirk from the hands of a small but thoroughly enraged mob. At precisely that moment Murdock formally arrested him for disturbing the peace, inciting a riot, mayhem and insurrection, and various and sundry lesser charges.

In spite of Officer Murdock's high state of alert readiness for such an occasion, Jacob Quirk offered no resistance of any kind. He came along peacefully and silently, a frustrating situation which caused the good policeman to confine his use of the nightstick to a few, furtive, but well-placed jabs, as they hurried away to the nearest precinct police station. Where, of course, the situation was promptly relieved, and in whose smoky rooms Murdock was able to get rid of his aggressions, believing, rightly, that pent-up resentment, aggression and hostility are as bad for health as constipation.

TWELVE

A fair and speedy trial

The magistrate was a man of some dignity and even more prestige. He had no aspiration to become Chief Justice. And he was not much amused.

"All right, smartass," he addressed the defendant. "Take off that silly *bleeping* beard."

"I believe it's a real one, Your Honor," Officer Murdock said.

"Correct, in a manner of speaking," Jacob Quirk added.

"Bailiff!"

The bailiff settled this problem of appearance and reality to the satisfaction of the black-robed magistrate by giving the said beard in question a few vigorous tugs. The combined phenomena of Quirk's howls and the fact that only a few stray hairs (and *these* with clearly evident roots)

69

came off in the bailiff's hands, were sufficient evidence.

"I guess one like this was bound to come along sooner or later," the magistrate said. "But why did it have to happen to me?"

He made a funny face, and everybody in the courtroom laughed appreciatively at the magistrate's sense of humor until he banged his gavel a few times to restore order.

Soon Officer Murdock took the stand. He testified with laudable accuracy and objectivity, describing the entire sequence of events, insofar as he had participated in or observed them. Next a couple of other eyewitnesses were called. They described, to the best of their recollection, a few of the choice and infuriating things which they had heard the defendant say as he spoke to them near the base of a statue. There was some disagreement about the statue. One witness swore it was a bronze equestrian representation of President Millard Fillmore. The other indignantly protested that it was a statue of the renowned British poet Arthur Hugh Clough. The defendant's court-appointed attorney seized upon this significant discrepancy and based his entire defense upon it. He was able to prove beyond a shadow of a doubt that the speech and the riot took place in front of a statue of Amie Semple Macpherson and that, as a matter of fact, the statue was a fair likeness of that famous evangelist whose career was, untimely, cut short.

"Have you anything to say before sentence is passed?" The magistrate asked the defendant. "And will you please give that sign to the Bailiff? The law expressly forbids advertising in the courtroom."

Jacob Quirk arose and, with all the gravity and dignity he could muster under the circumstances, addressed the Court.

"I was only trying to get across my message."

"And just what is your message?"

"That in whatever shape and form one finds himself, the one and only possible contentment accessible to a human being is to be at peace with oneself and to rejoice at being alive."

"It was that great American Samuel Goldwyn, I believe," the magistrate replied, "who so aptly said, 'If you gotta send a message, use the Western Union.'"

"Exception!" the defense attorney cried.

"Granted," the magistrate said. Then turning back to Quirk: "Tell me all about yourself."

Jacob Quirk began to recount the story of his life and his experiences. While he spoke, the magistrate seemed to be very interested, from time to time interrupting the narrative to ask for some detail or explanation. At one point he asked Quirk if he would care to give the Court a brief demonstration of his remarkable powers. Just for the record, so to speak.

Quirk nodded and smiled gratefully. He asked whom the magistrate would like to see him turn himself into.

"Napoleon," the magistrate said.

Apparently this was a kind of prearranged signal, for two guards raced forward and seized Quirk before he had even begun the comparatively simple process of shrinking and diminishing his height. And they clapped him sternly into a straitjacket before he had a chance to turn himself into Napoleon or anybody else. Thereupon he was half-dragged and half-carried to a prominent position directly in front of the magistrate's bench.

"This has been mighty interesting," the magistrate

71

said. "And I wish we could enjoy some more of your japes and pasquils. But it's getting close to my dinnertime."

He then gave Quirk a brief look, one which Quirk at once recognized as a passable imitation of the expression of pity, and ordered him to be committed and confined in the State Asylum for the Criminally Insane. This was to be considered an act of mercy, done as much for his own good as for the good of the State and the Society.

"You have to set me free!" Quirk shouted. "Because the whole world is an asylum for the criminally insane these days."

"I guess you've got a point there," the magistrate conceded as Quirk was carried away, lifted high, both feet furiously churning in thin air.

THIRTEEN

In the booby hatch

Once he became accustomed to the rules and the routine, the "drill," at the Insane Asylum, Jacob Quirk was able to relax and to enjoy the simple pleasures of the place. It was rather like (his memory told and consoled him) the State Orphans' Home where he had spent most of his childhood and youth—the same institutional furniture and feeling, the same institutional odors and noises, and much the same kind of food and drink. And here he found his companions much more entertaining and interesting. The pressures were slight; problems of any importance were few and far between. And it should not be forgotten—certainly Quirk did not forget—that he had a more than typical share of memories to comfort himself with.

Memory . . . He could, if he wanted to, remember all the human shapes and forms he had assumed. Of course, those forms, man or woman, beautiful or repulsive, young or old, had no experience or memory separate and distinct from his own. That had seemed a weakness in his art at the time, that he could not take on the treasure of a brand-new hive (and honey) of memories with each new form. But now he was glad that the forms had no existence but that which he had given them, namely his own. Otherwise he would have forgotten them each time he transformed himself.

Memory, true and false, no matter, was the best part of the self anyway, he decided. In memory all pleasures were the same—a warm, good feeling, here and now and very general. And all pains were painless, though the thought of them might make him uncomfortable and uneasy.

He shaved off his beard and trimmed his hair to conform to the institutional style. But he had no desire to return to his old form or, indeed, to practice his art in this place. At first, still outraged at the way the forces of Law and Justice had chosen to treat . . . not so much him, as his case, still a little bitter, he had gone so far as to do ordinary impersonations of the doctors, the staff, fellow patients, and especially in the context of the encounter group to which he had been assigned (briefly) for therapy. He got his revenge, together with a certain bearable remorse, by so annoying and distracting the young psychologist, who was the group leader, called "Trainer," that the poor fellow was required to undergo some treatment himself before he could be declared sane enough to leave both the Asylum and the profession for a quieter life pumping gas at a country filling station.

That was satisfactory, to be sure. Made Quirk feel better, even as he felt a little sorry for the fellow. Except, of

74

course, if he couldn't take the stress of simple impersonation, how could he have survived the whole thing, pure and naked transformation? Probably he was happy now with his gas pumps. They didn't make faces and talk back. They didn't make fun of him. Quirk concluded that he had, in his own way, helped the lad to *find himself*.

After that, he let well enough alone, enjoying the controlled and constant rehearsal of pleasant memories.

"I have lived a full, rich life," he would tell other people, anyone who would and could listen to him.

"Why don't you change yourself into one of the guards or nurses and walk right out? Why don't you get us all out of here?"

That was his friend speaking, his daily chess partner. He was not an exceptional master of chess, but he was a man absolutely convinced that he (and anyone else) could flap his arms in a certain vigorous, complex, methodical rhythm and thus become airborne and fly. He was so convinced of his theory that he had actually attempted to prove it on a number of occasions, with, unfortunately, negative results. The criminality of both his theory and the practice of it came from the fact that he had attempted to instruct others in the art, often against their will. His most notable pupil (she made front-page headlines on a relatively quiet day) was his own wife, whom he assisted on her initial takeoff out of a high hotel window. That lady had never been terribly fond of him and was even less enthralled by his original ideas. She had often scoffed at his theories, invariably comparing them in value and virtue to his *dingdong*—that is to say, short, limp and, in her best judgment and experience, worthless. And thus it was, after he had given her a final and marvelous opportunity to revise her point of view, that she refused to flap her arms even once during her long theatrical descent from the hotel window to the pavement far below. She made a good deal of noise, a long wailing series of obscenities uttered in thrilling diminuendo. But she refused to fly, just to spite him.

Jacob Quirk looked at his friend, smiled and shrugged.

"And why don't you get a running start and fly over the wall?"

"I really don't know, now that you mention it," his friend replied. "I could if I wanted to. But I suppose I kind of like it here. All my best friends are here, too."

"Exactly," Quirk said. "That's just the way I view the situation."

Aside from enjoying the company and the occasion to cultivate the garden of his memories, Quirk was, to all appearances, devastatingly sane. He passed all the latest psychological tests with flying colors. Some of his best friends in the Asylum were psychiatrists.

Eventually a time came when he was asked to appear before a distinguished board of doctors who would examine him and his case and then pass judgment on his future.

"How do you feel now?" he was asked.

"I feel just fine, thank you, sir."

"Aren't you still a little bit, even a teeny bit, hostile about being sent here?"

"I have no real complaints at all. I have decided that the magistrate was fair and just. I probably would have done the same thing if the situation had been different and our respective positions had been reversed. He did what he had to do, what the Law and the circumstances required. And, of course, he was, just as we all are, caught like a fly in the web of himself and his own limitations. The truth is, I wish him well."

"Is there anything particular you would like to talk to us about?"

"Not really," Quirk answered. "I have a number of things I'd like to discuss, but I suppose I'll have to wait."

"Why?"

"God is the one I want to talk to."

The learned doctors looked at each other quickly, exchanging brief, bleak, professional shrugs. Several of them were compelled to bend over and scribble notes.

"What is it you want to discuss with God?"

"I just want Him to know that I have thought it all over and decided that He is fair too," Quirk said. "I want Him to understand that I am ready to forgive Him for everything, if He'll do the same for me."

"I am sure He will be very pleased to hear that," the Chairman of the Board said, nodding to the guards at the door. "Send in the next one."

FOURTEEN

Final excerpt from Quirk's Journal

Poets, existentialists, psychiatrists, friends and relatives to the contrary, this is not necessarily the best place to be.

You can take it from me.

All things considered, the loony bin leaves a lot to be desired.

True, all the world's more like a funny farm than a Broadway stage. You'll notice that much right away, if you care enough to take a hard, unblinking look at it (the world) instead of minding your own beeswax.

True, all the world's a mental hospital, and we are only patients in it etc. etc. etc., as some of those intellectual French existentialists are forever and a day asserting. And whacking out, going stark, nose-thumbing, finger-licking, bareass raving mad may, indeed, yes, sir!, represent one of the two remaining choices by which your average fellow can prove his freedom and enjoy his own brand of poison. The other choice, according to these philosophers, being suicide. Which still strikes me as an extreme way to prove a logical point. And I can't help but notice that most of *them*, I mean the bigshot, fulltime, professional existentialists, either have died in bed or at least look like a shoo-in to make it that way, clean and natural. It's their disciples, literal-minded kids who couldn't tell a metaphor if it bit them, who are running to the pharmacies to buy super-keen new razor blades and fancy and final prescriptions, or else lining up at the hardware stores to try and get a good deal on a short piece of stout rope.

That's their problem.

True, just like any other institution, the Crazyhouse is a self-serving system, a self-perpetuating outfit, designed to give people, from psychiatrists to janitors, some useful work to do and to serve the "patients" three meals a day and to keep you more or less alive for as long as reasonably possible.

True enough, they will leave you pretty much alone once they decide that you are either incurable or not worth the trouble. And, either way, that gives you a lot of free, leisure time on your hands.

Which is great, at least at first. Except that with leisure time, you always end up thinking. The old mind just keeps going along, clickety-clack, beepty-beep, and rat-a-tat-tat. Now, you can try, as I have been doing, and stick to memory. Just go floating off in a nice lukewarm tub of nostalgia. Or if that doesn't grab you, you can plan for a future that will never be. Or you can phase out and into the never-never territory of Fantasyland. Any of these three separately or all at once.

But, when you consider it rationally, that is hardly any improvement at all over sanity. Same old crock . . .

Maybe I am just blue.

I hate being downhearted and downbeat.

No doubt there is some reasonable explanation for my feelings of depression.

For one thing, I miss my former chess partner.

Yes, he finally decided to give it the old college try. He was going to try it even though he was fully aware that the long period of inactivity might have left him rusty.

You have got to give him credit for a lot of guts.

At breakfast—they served those crummy Frostie Flakies again!—he announced his intention.

"Okay, okay," he said. "Enough is enough, and I am leaving."

"No kidding?"

"*Blanking*-A!" He said. "Why don't you come with me?"

"I can't fly for sour apples. And I don't have time to learn."

"True, all too true. It takes time to master my art. But you can always turn yourself into somebody, maybe the garbageman, and then meet me on the other side of the wall."

"It's been a while," I said. "I'm kind of out of shape."

"So am I," he said. "Besides, I never *really* tried it, not the whole routine, even when I was in the pink. But I know it will work."

"I wish you wouldn't."

"Why? Don't you believe in me?"

"I'd like to. I really would."

"Listen, smarty pants, do you want to make a little

wager on this? You want to put some money where your big mouth is?"

"Please don't get yourself excited."

"Put up or shut up!"

"I'm sorry," I said. "I never bet against my friends."

"What's wrong with you, Jacob? Are you crazy or something?"

"Well, I can't be certain about that," I said. "But it's a distinct possibility that one of us is as nutty as an Almond Joy."

"Oh yeah? We'll see who's nuts around here. We'll see about that!"

Whereupon he dumped over his untouched bowl of Frostie Flakies, jumped up on the table and ran the length of it, greatly disturbing the other kooks who were trying to eat. He was flapping his arms and cawing a crowlike sound.

Guards came running and cussing. But they were so busy swinging their bruiseless, but painful truncheons (we call it "discipline therapy" here) that, though they succeeded in evoking several cries of pain and rage from him, they couldn't catch him. He eluded them.

And he ran right out of the dining hall and outside across the big exercise yard towards the chapel.

I'll say this, at a dead run that guy looked like he could fly if he ever got off the ground. There isn't a guard in the place who could keep up with him on a sprint. I have no idea how he would have done at cross-country or a distance race.

Anyway, he reached the chapel well ahead of his pursuers and managed to get inside the bell tower and to lock and bolt the big doors behind him.

He rang the bells like a . . . well, like a madman, if you must, for maybe a half hour or so to gain everybody's attention. Even the psychiatrists took note that the persistent clanging and ringing were real. Some of them came out to join the crowd and watch.

Suddenly the ringing stopped, and he soon appeared on top of the bell tower, the highest spot on the Asylum grounds. He was as naked as a newborn babe, and he was trying, or so it seemed, to address the crowd below. But everybody in the crowd was yelling at him at once. And even if they hadn't been, the noise of the telephone pole, which they were using as a battering ram to break down the door, would have drowned out his words.

So, with an eloquent, bare-shouldered shrug, and taking his cue from the chapel's traditional weathervane, he cried out, loud and clear, "Cock-a-doodle-doo!" And he began to flap his arms in a beautiful rhythm. And then he launched himself into the air.

There has been a lot of talk around the Asylum ever since then, about just how far he actually flew. In the wards this has been the subject of some heated arguments and even fistfights. Some witnesses maintain that he had achieved a good clean takeoff and was in level flight when one of the tower guards shot him down like a dove. I believe that the witnesses who claim this are probably mistaken. They misconstrued the loud crack of the bell tower door giving way to the battering ram and assumed that it was a rifle report.

In any case, regardless of whose testimony you prefer to believe, which version you accept, it is a fact that he did not fly very far before he went into a distinct stall and tailspin, then fell like a watermelon onto the asphalt of the parking lot, just managing to miss hitting the Chaplain's Porsche, which was parked there.

Well, anyway, I feel pretty bad about it. Maybe if I had said yes, and then, for example, publicly and miserably failed to turn myself into anyone but Jacob Quirk in his blue, booby-hatch pajamas, he wouldn't have been so competitive and rash.

Who knows?

All I know for sure is I lost a fairly good chess partner. Most of the other clods around here can't concentrate long enough to play out a game. Or they *won't* concentrate. They are, like most average bedlamites, stubborn and willful and crafty. They are not to be trusted.

Still, I do not despair. All is not lost.

I can't put it all down here in the *Journal*, where some half-baked, lame-brain shrink might find it and try to use it against me. But nevertheless . . . Nevertheless, something very interesting happened to me last night. And when it did, I started thinking that I might make something out of myself yet.

We'll see what we shall see.

The thing is, I was wrong. I had never really thought it through before. Back in the old days, on the outside, I was so busy performing and practicing my craft that I lost sight of the implications, the ultimate ends and goals of my art form.

Here is how it dawned on me. After they turned the lights out, I lay there in my sack just listening to the music of snores, coughs, farts and groans, produced by the assorted crazies in the ward. I just lay still, listening, and feeling bad about the unfortunate demise of my high-flying friend.

I should have been a mongrel dog or something, I told myself.

And then it came. Just like a lightbulb in a comic strip. Right then and there I realized that all along I had been ignoring an important artistic possibility. By inadvertently and ignorantly limiting both my impersonations and transformations to the human being. What the hell?, I reasoned, an ape wouldn't be too hard. After that? Well, dogs and cats, pigs and deer, snakes and birds etc. would present some real problems and challenges. But these would not be insurmountable ones.

So I lay there, in a warm and pleasing glow of penance and atonement, imagining myself transformed into an ugly, mangy, old, half-blind, mongrel dog slinking along the sidewalk of the city. I saw myself dodging feet and automobiles, looking for something. Looking for a . . . fire hydrant.

I found a hydrant, sniffed around it, stopped, poised, hoisted up a hind leg dramatically and . . .

Wait a minute, I told myself. Right idea, all right. Right image. Wrong role.

I laughed out loud picturing myself as a fire hydrant. And yet a man could do and could be worse. Fire hydrants serve other purposes. They are used to put out fires, to make summer afternoons bearable for the city's kids. They are very convenient for fat men to use when they have to tie their shoes. They add to public revenue and general welfare, because people are always leaving their cars next to hydrants and getting parking tickets for it.

Why on earth have I confined my art and craft, limited it to so-called living things?

New possibilities of pop art presented themselves to

me in a flash. Your run-of-the-mill pop artist can turn out fake Campbell Soup cans and Brillo boxes, sure. But I, the Prince of Impersonators, I should be able to *be* either one. Or anything else I want to be.

Talk about the possibilities of atonement!

But no good ever comes from guilt or feeling guilty. Guilt is so transient, anyway. When it becomes too heavy, too painful to bear, we react by transferring it to the nearest available and vulnerable human being.

The more I think about this, the more I am convinced that this is as things ought to be.

The world's a game of tag. It's all complex and marvelous, a wild game combining tag, keep away, and hide and seek.

Button, button, who's got the button? What if I *am* the button? Then how do you play?

One thing for sure, the best thing, and probably our bounden duty, is to run free and, when caught, not to remain "it" any longer than absolutely necessary.

And so it dawned upon me, even as another literal dawn was coming on to give the rosy finger to all of us poor creeps in this snakepit, that I had let myself be "it" for far too long. I had practically broken the great chain of being. I had almost lost my human nature in the process.

Well, sir, we shall see about that.

We'll see about that, now, won't we?

Don't worry about me. Just look for me where you find me.

FIFTEEN

Quirk's masterpiece

Frankly, nobody has a clue as to what finally became of Jacob Quirk. Or—to put it another way and to give him the benefit of some credulity—nobody knows what he became. If he became anything . . .

We have his crazy *Journal*, of course. That is, we will have it in due time and due course. It is presently reported to be safe in the National Archives, safe and classified; for there seem to be some items in it which concern the national security. Perhaps—why not?—at some stage of his earlier career, during the human transformation stage, he could have turned himself into some politician or diplomat, *even* (let us admit the possibility and the dangers of it) the President of the United States and/or his rivals. It would only require *one* caper of this kind to cause a great deal of mischief on a global scale. And we have to allow that such a thing *could* have happened. (So do our allies and enemies.) There have been strange turns and counterturns in our political life over the past years. It would be easy to blame Quirk for all of them. Still, may we not consider that he could have been responsible for some of the weirdo, strango things that our leaders seem to have done? Sooner or later the *Journal* will be declassified, and then we can satisfy our curiosity.

We can (when we get to see more than the excerpts of it) believe the *Journal* if we care to. Or we can believe some parts of it, all the while vehemently denying the truth of other parts. Or we can give a big thumbs down and a fluttering and sloppy Bronx cheer to the whole *bleeping* thing, claiming that, at most, it is just another half-baked example of modern American fiction and about as credible (not more, not less) as, say, *The Warren Report*, or as sincere as the *Tonkin Gulf Resolution*. Or, if we wish, perhaps wisely, to avoid taking any stand or making any comparisons that might get us into trouble, we can safely say that it looks just like the kind of thing that some crazy, misanthropic writer would dream up, the kind of a guy who is so far out of it that he is practically a Quirk himself.

Somebody could make a case (and somebody probably will) for the fact that Jacob Quirk himself—in person, so to speak—never existed at all. Except, of course, in the fevered and degenerate imagination of the aforesaid imaginary writer, or, more likely his publisher, since most books are totally and completely the creations of publishers, except, of course, for the actual typing, which is where the writer comes in.

Be that as it may, there are some things which seem to be fairly certain.

One morning there was an empty and unmade cot in the ward where Quirk claimed he lived. And, as well, there were the previously mentioned *Journal*, some clothes, a portable chess set, and a pipe and tobacco. The pipe and tobacco might be suspect. Until now they have never been mentioned before. But, before jumping to any conclusions, please pause to consider this. How do you imagine Jacob Quirk, *with* or *without* a pipe? It wouldn't (except that time he was pretending to be a rich man) be a big cigar. A pipe seems appropriate, don't you think?

Anyway, there is the undeniably unmade and empty cot with a label affixed to the foot of it: QUIRK, JACOB— PARANOID/SCHIZO, 8763 494.

The Chief Psychiatrist is a white-haired, rosy-cheeked, jowly, smiling Santa Claus gent with a cute German accent, who never seems to lose his authentic Old World charm or to blow his cool. Except when somebody is dumb enough or rude enough to bring up the 1940s. Which he argues, most persuasively, never really happened, in his brilliant contribution to revisionist history—*The Lost Decade of the Forties: A Study in Mass Hallucination*. The Chief Psychiatrist, Dr. Smartheim, argues that Jacob Quirk, too, was an hallucination, a mere "experiment" as it were, carefully devised and perpetrated upon the highly suggestible, criminal nuts in his charge.

He's got a point. The only people at the Asylum who claim to have seen Jacob Quirk are some of the patients.

The success of "The Quirk Experiment," as Smartheim calls it (see his report in *Modern Lunacy*, XIV, ii, pp. 113–26), is a preliminary indication, initial evidence of a plausible hypothesis that a great many public figures are only mass hallucinations, the products of the corrupt and decadent mass consciousness of our times.

He may be right about that, too. Jacob Quirk could have told him that much while he was still a nightclub and cabaret performer.

From the above hypothesis, it could follow that a very large part of what is called human history is really nothing more than a sort of dream, a bad dream at that. This is a point which many distinguished philosophers, poets, theologians, and even some politicians and military leaders, have been suggesting down through the ages, in a metaphorical if not a literal sense. The validity of the Smartheim theory remains to be seen. We wait upon a research project in depth, headed up by Smartheim and funded by the National Endowment for the Humanities and several of the larger foundations.

In any event, at this time it is quite impossible to determine and to prove, without prompt refutation, that Jacob Quirk ever existed. It is equally difficult to prove that he did not exist and does not exist now, at the moment of this writing. Significantly, the burden of proof is upon Quirk himself.

Which makes it even more difficult. Assume that a man calling himself Jacob Quirk, insisting that he is Quirk, should appear and choose to confront the eminent Dr. Smartheim. That might be a rash thing to do; for, with a stroke of his pen, the distinguished Doctor could have the wretch committed, for "observation" at the least, perhaps even for "treatment and therapy." The results of that kind of attention and scrutiny might easily persuade the gentleman in question that he is not and never has been

Jacob Quirk at all, but is, instead (for example), Attila the Hun, Little Black Sambo, or the Ghost of Xmas Past.

In short, friendly Reader, the truth about Jacob Quirk—the truth, the whole truth, and nothing but—seems predetermined to remain unresolved.

Nevertheless, there are some curious incidents which, though not yet in any direct and tangible way linked to Quirk, reality or fiction, are necessary to report and consider. I mention them, not out of a desire to "make a case" one way or the other, nor out of any interest in blatant sensationalism, but chiefly out of deference to the considerable number of people ("Quirk jerks," as Smartheim calls them) who seem to believe that Jacob Quirk is for real. Far be it from me to fly in the face of any consensus of opinion, even a minority opinion.

People point to any number of inexplicable incidents and events, as frequent and as debatable as the sightings of UFOs in our skies, as proof. Some of the "Quirk jerks" believe Quirk *is* a UFO, thus solving two problems at once and with neatness and dispatch. Others mention the popular mystery surrounding that hairy and perhaps abominable humanoid called Bigfoot and said to stalk the remote forests and mountainous areas of northern California and western Canada. Hollywood types may jokingly claim that Bigfoot is really the ghost of the late great picture maker Harry Cohn. But that kind of joke is in bad taste and solves nothing.

However, most of the things cited by these obsessed "believers" in the Quirk myth have some logical explanation. A distinguished Commission, appointed by the President and composed of scientists, judges, shipping magnates, steel tycoons, labor and civil rights leaders, movie stars, priests, preachers, rabbis, and the family and relatives of leaders of Congress, has been in almost continuous session for some time, drawing a *per diem* allowance and sifting the evidence as they prepare a report which may someday be made public. Their final conclusion and judgment must remain a matter of conjecture until that happy day. But even now, through entirely reliable, though necessarily anonymous sources, it is possible to report on some of their findings.

First, practically all these odd incidents have some satisfactory explanation in no way connected with Jacob Quirk. And ninety-nine out of a hundred of them, conservatively, may be dismissed out of hand.

Such ludicrous and celebrated examples as the Dirty Talking Taxicab of New York City; the obscene neon sign which appeared atop the Golden Gate Bridge; the champagne which suddenly filled the pipes of the Public Water System of Temperance, Iowa, and as suddenly disappeared, replaced by a noxious and sulphurous artesian brew; the Spanish Fly which somehow was bottled in the Pepsi-Cola served in the machines at Vassar College, and caused all *that* unfortunate excitement; the showing in Cherokee, N.C., of the film *The Sound of Music* during which the principals appeared (to the stunned audience, at least) completely in the nude and performing lewd and indecent acts; the nationally televised appearance of the New York City Ballet Company during which millions of viewers claim to have seen a macabre and grotesque "dance" by a group equally divided between cannibals and vegetarian victims—all these, and others of their ilk, have some kind of explanation and can be discarded here and now and forever as not having any significance whatsoever.

"In large part, these and other absurdities," the Committee report will state, "are what may be called mere statistical aberrations. After all, statistically, if millions of monkeys were placed before millions of typewriters, sooner or later one of them would inevitably type out *The Complete Works of William Shakespeare.* Which is not to imply that the plays of Shakespeare were written by a monkey. However attractive that thought may be, there is irrefutable evidence that Shakespeare's plays represent a rare collaboration between Francis Bacon and Edward Coke. And, in any case, though there *were* some monkeys in Elizabethan England, there is no evidence that a sufficient number of them existed there for the optimum conditions of statistical probability to be sufficient. Moreover, lacking a notion of progress or any real desire for technical improvement, those underdeveloped people in that era had not yet imagined, let alone invented, the typewriter."

It is reliably reported that the Quirk Commission will exonerate Dr. Smartheim and tentatively conclude that Jacob Quirk probably was an hallucination.

Nevertheless, in the interests of objectivity and fair play, the Commission will acknowledge and offer no comment upon a number of small, insignificant, and as yet unexplained events. These, inconsequential as they may be, are still clung to, like relics, by the "Quirk jerks."

There is the matter of Dr. Smartheim's golden fountain pen.

There seems to be no doubt that shortly after Quirk "disappeared," Dr. Smartheim began to have considerable difficulty in controlling a gold fountain pen which Mrs. Smartheim gave him for the purpose of writing up the results of a number of experiments. Smartheim has nothing against the typewriter or modern technology generally, but he prefers to do his writing with a fountain pen because, as he has said, "I don't like machinery to get between me and the creative words on the page."

However, *something* seems to have come between Smartheim and the words he wanted to put down on pages while he was using the gold fountain pen.

The first thing he noticed was the not atypical writer's difficulty of almost instinctively choosing exactly the wrong word at the center of some key passage of his work. Somehow, suddenly and without warning, an outrageous adjective or a hoodlum adverb would pop onto the page from the moving point of his pen, not only ruining the entire context, but also interrupting his train of thought, like Lawrence of Arabia blowing up a locomotive. By the time he had collected himself, the subtle *gestalt* of his rhetoric was strictly *kaput*. He made nothing of this at first, surmising it to be a form of "writer's block." Since this surmise could be subjected to experiment and inquisition, he arranged things so that the next time a prominent poet or novelist flipped out of his tree and went wiggy, the artist would be committed to his care for observation. Smartheim alerted friends and agents from coast to coast to be on the lookout for crazy writers he could use as subjects. And that is how the Smartheim Institute for Literary Behavior began. Already the Institute has had more prominent poets and novelists in residence than the rolls of the American Academy of Arts and Letters. Indeed, as all but the most unsophisticated readers must know, a sojourn in the Institute has become a badge of status in the literary establishment.

But therein hangs another tale, another story not directly relevant to the mystery of the gold fountain pen.

This exceptional pen, as he might have expected, asserted its independence openly, shamelessly, arrogantly. It made a mockery of the very memos he scribbled, a snowstorm of paper "From Smartheim's Couch," to keep his staff reeling with an awareness of who was the bossman. It also, apparently, introduced spurious and unattractive details into a private diary Smartheim was keeping to record the condition of his own mental health.

Why, for example, did the gold pen insist on signing letters and documents with "Smartheim the Superkraut"?

Why did the pen insult a distinguished member of his staff, a well-known psychiatrist, calling him a "crummy pinko kike" and further suggesting that his greatest value would be as "a bar of soap"?

Why did the pen, of its own volition, from time to time write out in bold, block, capital letters, "SMARTHEIM AIN'T TELLING NOBODY WHERE *HE* WAS IN 1944"?

Why did the pen persist in doodling in his notebook, while he listened to patients spilling their guts, such irreverent things as "Fooey on Freud"?

No one can answer these questions. All we know is that Smartheim destroyed the pen by jumping up and down on it, on top of his desk during a staff meeting. The offending remnants were buried in quicklime.

Asked about these extraordinary precautions, Smartheim has answered:

"Of course it was not this Quirk. Quirk never existed. He was a mere figment. However, just in case, in the unlikely event he ever *did* exist and seized control of my fountain pen, he learned his lesson. Don't *blank* around with Smartheim or you will get hurt bad, that's the moral. I really fixed that bastard and he will never be heard of again. When figments get out of line, you have to be firm with them. That's what they want anyway. Figments, in general, need directive treatment and are happier in their own place."

Another "mystery" worthy of mention concerns an unusual clock which was once the proud possession of a theatrical agent. Here, thanks to a friendly anonymous source, we have in hand an exact transcript of the statement made by this individual, under oath, to the Quirk Commission.

That statement, slightly edited to facilitate reading, is as follows:

"May it please you, honorable ladies and gentlemen of the Commission . . . I am only a poor and humble agent, a servant for many talented men and women in the worlds of Entertainment, Show Biz, and the Seven Lively Arts. I know that there are those people who speak badly of agents as a group, putting the knock on us as greedy and lazy parasites who do nothing and then collect ten per cent or sometimes more of the so-called artists' hard-earned money. They sometimes call us gangsters, hustlers, confidence men and worthless clods. But they do not know you-know-what from Shinola. Artists are very temperamental and ungrateful and frequently lacking in any talent whatsoever. They also tend to lack humility, these egotistical, arrogant, so-called artists. Without agents they would be nothing! Bums in the park, that's what they would be! Or filling up the jails, the booby hatches and the morgues. Not only do we agents do them great service, by arranging for them to have an opportunity to practice their so-called arts at the public's expense, but also—if I may say so in all modesty—we are patriots who save our country much trouble. We keep these lazy, no-account rascals and rogues off the streets and the welfare rolls where they probably belong, but where they would surely bankrupt the government at state, local, and federal levels. It has been argued by some of my colleagues in the agent vocation that by logic and by right we, the agents, deserve at least a ten per cent cut of the Gross National Product for our good works. Be that as it may, I do not think it is fair that we should be subject to constant harassment and surveillance by the moronic minions of the Internal Revenue Service, who do not understand the complex nature of our business and are only living and waxing fat off of our excessive taxes anyway.

"Agents—except for IRS agents—are useful and valuable citizens of this great land. It has always seemed practically ironic to me, if you'll pardon the expression, that agents, who are, after all, simple and honest businessmen, capitalistic to the core, should be held up for ridicule while any deadbeat who can play the piano or paint a picture or swallow a sword should receive applause and accolades, cash and kudos, from one and all. After every performance, after every exhibition or show, the so-called artists should modestly retire to the rotten woodwork from whence they came, and the agent should step forward to take the bows.

"But, honorable sirs and ladies, let us leave philosophy to the professionals and get to the business at hand. I know your time is valuable, and so is mine. Time is valuable to everyone except those so-called artists who lounge and

97

slouch around loafing and inviting their souls, as a poet, himself a self-confessed bum, once urged everyone to do.

"It is true that at one time I handled the worthless human being who was billed as 'Proteus, Prince of Impersonators.' To the best of my recollection he also called himself Jacob Quirk. But this may be pure confluence, not to say coincidence. For in Show Biz, there be few if any (if the truth be known) that give their right name.

"Here just let me ad lib and say right out without shame that my name is not really Irving Schmertz. I would rather not reveal my legal name, if you don't mind, and I won't ask you yours. Which looks to me, honorables, like a Mexican standoff, if not a fair deal. Suffice it to say that when I prepared myself for my vocation I noticed that all the most successful agents were named Irving or variations thereof such as Irvin, Erwin, or Irwin etc. Schmertz was suggested to be my first secretary, who noted that it sounded good and original and that it seemed to fit somehow.

"That was good enough for me, gentlemen. Sometimes a thing just *feels* right and you cannot explain why. That is because Show Biz is a mystical thing.

"Anyhow, I handled this individual who called himself Jake. What was he? A punk kid who could make faces, that's all. I made a star of him, put his name in neon lights and all that. But he was strictly a nothing from beginning to end. And I do not for one minute believe all this . . . well, *stuff* about turning himself into other people and all that. That sounds like some second-rate drunken flack, or a press agent as we call them. Jake was too stupid and conceited even to think of the idea.

"Nevertheless, before he lost his mind and his humility, I handled him well. Right up there in the big time. And we got along all right except for arguments about money. He never could understand all the extra expenses and overhead it costs to make a nobody into a star and keep him there. It did no good to show him the facts and figures. He would go over them with a fine-toothed comb and yell and scream about everything, even minor mistakes in addition and subtraction. And that was something from a guy who could not even add two and two on his own.

"He was a reckless spender too, among other deviant and antisocial things. He also wore wide neckties long before they were correct again.

"To understand this thing, gentlemen and ladies, you got to understand I am sort of a demon about time. Time is as precious as blood and energy in my business. Time is almost as important as money. With clients coming and going all the time and phones ringing constantly, I live by a tight schedule and I have to watch the clock.

"Which is how I became a kind of clock buff, started collecting the things and stashing them all over my office in prominent places. Not only for my own purposes, but also so that no matter where a client turned he would see a clock working, ticking off my valuable time. I collected some pretty fine clocks of all kinds, if I do say so myself, and I kept them all synchronized and in perfect working order. Naturally, when the hour struck it was noisy, as you can imagine, in my office, damn near deafening with all those chimes and bells and clonks and booms. But I had my earplugs ready. Which muted the noise and also cut off the sound of the clients' voices. And usually scared the stuffing out of them. For as the hour approached I was wont to distract them from observing the clocks by words and gestures, and I only slipped in the earplugs at the last possible second. Mostly they were taken by surprise and then scared witless, affording me an opportunity for a good hearty laugh at least once every hour.

"A man without a sense of humor is only half civilized, I always say.

"Well, to make a long story short, ladies and gentlemen, one day I received a package in the mail. Since it was ticking and since I have known many disgruntled and degenerate clients in my time and even a few jealous competitors, and since I have two ex-wives who were so crushed at my walking out on them that they have been half crazy ever since, not to mention secretaries and some young ladies who, as a result of the most casual and informal encounters, seem to feel that they have some claim against me, for all these reasons, I instantly called the Bomb Disposal Squad.

"However, it was not a bomb at all. It was a beautiful and highly original clock. Judging by its works, I would say early nineteenth century. But I am not a real expert. It was a big heavy clock in a finely made case with a gold dome on top. It had four different kinds of chimes, all swell-sounding, and on the hour two figures came out, two knights, one a black knight with a curved sword and the other a white man with a red cross on his armor and a big spiked mace. The black knight would swing the sword and miss every time. Whitey would then clout his skull with the mace, striking the hour resoundingly.

"I thought it was a gas and so did most of my other clients, except, of course, the colored. Who are very touchy and uppity these days, as I guess everyone knows.

"With the clock came a card—I have it here—which says: 'To Irving the Great/From a Client Who Will Never Forget.'

"I was deeply moved by those sentiments, ladies and gentlemen.

"Nine times out of ten, they leave shaking their fists and talking loud and rude. And you never hear from them again. Here at last, thought I, was one who had cooled off enough to understand.

"I was touched, deeply moved, and sincerely grateful. But, oh, was I in for it! Little did I know . . .

"One day when the clock was about to strike noon and I was getting ready to cut out for a meaningful luncheon with a prominent producer, the big black knight swung that curved razor and cut off the red-cross knight's head before he could even swing a blow with the mace. I could hardly believe my eyes. Or my ears either. Even though I had my earplugs firmly seated, I swear I heard that coon holler "Black Power, you Mother-*blanker!*" twelve times before he gave me the finger and vanished back into the clock.

"Very candidly, I felt terrible about that. It almost ruined my luncheon for me.

"But that was only the beginning. In the first place, after that all kinds of figures came out instead of the knights, usually in pairs and up to no good whatsoever. The things they would say and do I shudder to think of, let alone repeat.

"I guess the most *costly* was when I was just about to get this high-priced leading lady to dump her old agent and sign on the dotted line with me. Well, I carefully arranged it so she would miss the hour and, to make double sure, I let the evil clock run down and didn't even wind it. A lot of good that did. Just when she picked up my pen to sign the contract, the thing started booming and chiming like crazy. We both looked up, naturally, just in time to see two nude figures come out on the platform. One was a dead ringer for the leading lady in question. The other, I am sorry to say, was a pretty fair representation of yours truly in a state of nature and, shall we say, somewhat aroused. I was shocked to see what happened.

"When it was all over, she was furious. She poured a bottle of ink over my head and wadded up the contract and stuffed it into my open mouth, for I was protesting my innocence vehemently, and she left my office vowing never to darken my door again.

"Unfortunately, for once in her worthless life, the lady kept her word.

"That was typical. And the finest clockmakers in the city couldn't locate the trouble. In fact, they couldn't find out what the trouble was. Every time a clock expert came around that damn clock behaved perfectly. Trying to make me look like a fool.

"But that was not the worst part. That evil clock corrupted every other clock and watch I owned. None of them kept the correct time or even the same time. I got to where I couldn't tell night from day.

"And lots of them began, without warning or rhyme or reason, to sound off with 'Cuckoo! Cuckoo! Irving is a Cuckoo!,' not only on the hour but whenever they felt like it.

"Well, honorable sirs and ma'ms, enough is enough. Even the patience and goodwill of an agent isn't inexhaustible. Therefore one day I borrowed a fireman's ax and I chopped that clock into little bitty pieces. And put the pieces in a sack and drove out to a remote place in the country. I burned the clock and the works to ashes and I urinated upon the ashes of it.

"Which is how and why I had that unfortunate misunderstanding with the local police who happened along about that time and, lacking the necessary background information, jumped to erroneous conclusions.

"But I bear them no grudge.

"I don't bear the ungrateful ex-client who called himself Jake Quirk any grudge either. If there is such a person and he is somewhere today, I say unto him: 'Jake, I am willing to let bygones be bygones. I am willing to call it even-Stephen. It was a good trick, Jake. I'll give you full credit. But please, Jake, please, I will be profoundly grateful to you if you will be so kind as to pick on somebody else and leave me alone.'

"Thank you very much for your attention, ladies and gentlemen. I'll give you the same anytime. Drop into my office and see if I don't. My door is always open."

The rest must be speculation and lies beyond the proper limits of critical inquiry. The various followers of and true believers in Quirk are mostly congregated in and around the two licensed Temples of Proteus in the Los Angeles area. They have theories as to where The Master has been and what he may be up to now.

The most extreme views are held by a small band of shaggy, unsmiling young men who attend neither temple and picket both. They call themselves "The Latter Day Congregation of Proteus, The Anarchist." They do not give interviews often, and when the spokesman for the group does talk to interested strangers, he will only discuss generalities.

The spokesman for the group implies that The Master is even now active and busy all over the world, causing the kinds of sorrow and troubles that human beings deserve.

"Since nothing will ever bring them to their senses," he says, "The Master is using a radical approach at last. He is driving them *out* of their senses, such senses as they still possess. Once the whole world is wiggy, then we can start all over again."

At The Temple of the Primitive Proteus on Sunset Boulevard, an acolyte pauses for a moment during the lighting of the candles. He looks at me with a soulful, beatific, and somehow condescending expression.

"No one knows where The Master may be at this time," he tells me. "He is everywhere and he is nowhere, dig? He is the candle, he is the flame, he is the smoke. You dig that?"

"Come on, do you really believe that?"

He grins. He looks around, then takes me aside, into the shadows, to whisper in my ear.

"What I think—now don't repeat this or write it down or anything, because it could cost me my job around here—right now he is up in the belly of a B-52 bomber. *They* think he is just an ordinary hydrogen bomb with all these safety features, see? But secretly he has turned himself into a cobalt bomb. And, man, he is just laying there, cooling it, waiting for the right time to go off. You know what happens when a cobalt bomb goes up, don't you? *Zap!* The whole freaking world goes with it. *Finto, kaput,* the end! And, you know what?, I can hardly wait. I mean, a lot of slobs around this temple are in for a big surprise."

The more conservative and respectable Temple of Protean Mysteries, located in Beverly Hills, is much less violent in its rhetoric. In fact, the Bishop (formerly a successful practitioner of Zen acupuncture in "civilian" life), only smiles at these heresies.

"You must try to understand," he says. "The Master lived a full and active life, touching upon all facets of experience. And the clear message of his story is a simple one—in any shape or form human life is a disease. It follows, then, as certain as dawn follows the darkest night and as sure as the Good Creator made little green apples, that the truly Protean life, which is the only true life possible, is interior. It is a life of passive contemplation.

"We look with awe and reverence upon the events of his life, as they are revealed in the *Journal*, for example; but we are not misled by these things. By which I mean to say that The Master is more to be understood and to be judged by what he did not do than by anything he may have done or become.

"We look upon The Master's life and his thoughts as a testament, call it a gospel if you wish, of the immutable, ineffable, and eternal truth of the inner life. Crucified, as it were, upon the cross of crude appearances, he has triumphed over the seeming reality of the world and proved that it is false.

"Such modern problems of the moment, for example such fashionable pseudo problems as personal 'identity crises' or 'alienation,' or war and peace, pollution and poverty and political corruption, and so forth and so on, all these things can now be seen and known for what they are—diversions, distractions, snares and delusions to the spirit.

"We are liberated from such things. Stripped naked, our separate and sexless spirits join hands in an endless and invisible dance. . . .

"But I do not expect you to understand all of this or to begin to believe, not so long as you are still so much a prisoner of appearances that you must come to me in search of knowledge and understanding."

Tolerant, smiling, he offered me a cigarette, lit it and his own with a curiously elegant gold cigarette lighter. We smoked and sipped tea in silence. I found my eyes drawn to the kaleidoscopic patterns of gold and silver thread set in the luminous silk of his robe.

"We have these made by a little man in Hong Kong," he said. "They are not half as expensive as they look."

He gestured with his long-nailed hands.

"You must realize that it is of no consequence to us, the faithful, whether or not The Master really 'existed.' What you call existence is at best no more than a dream to be forgotten. To insist upon what you call facts, historical credibility, would be to deny the very heart of our faith. Therefore we do not concern ourselves with such matters. But we are still free to imagine him as we choose to."

"Well, sir, if that is so . . ."

"It is so. No doubt about it."

"Yes, sir. Well . . . what do you imagine will become of him?"

"Who knows?" the Bishop said. "Perhaps—it would seem to be fitting and proper—perhaps The Master, having accomplished his great mission, is prepared to withdraw and to settle into one final shape. Perhaps he will turn into this book you are writing."

"Do you really think so?"

"Why not?"

Noise of Strangers

A story

Thou shalt bring down the noise of
strangers, as the heat in a dry place;
even the heat with the shadow of a
cloud; the branch of the terrible ones
shall be brought low.

ISAIAH 25:5

Larry Berlin is driving north on Route 27 when he spots the car. It is a new white Plymouth convertible going too fast. No more than a sudden bright dazed smear of shine and chrome against the monotonous gray of the dawn. Any other time and he probably would let it go, let the car go by and on, to hell or safety for all he cares, rather than slowing down to stop and then turning around, which means having to doodlebug here with a ditch and dense pine woods on both sides of the road and neither a trail nor a footpath to nose into.

It may be nothing more to him at this moment than a wince of surprise after long, slow, boring night hours, the surprise of now rounding a wide curve and coming almost face to face with a shimmering apparition of pure speed when he had every reason to look for only the yawn of the empty highway ahead of him. Or, maybe, it is something more. An abrupt, utterly thoughtless, visceral knowledge of danger. Danger and challenge. Whatever it is that warns and alerts him, he does not waste one second to make up his mind. He twists the wheel sharply to avoid the collision. He slows down and brakes. In two smooth motions, he doodlebugs his car, and now he is off in the other direction in pursuit, his foot jamming the gas pedal down to the floor board. He can feel a slow easy grin begin to take command of his lips as he grips the steering wheel tight and leans well forward. Like a jockey.

Whether he is now really gaining or it is only that the Plymouth has started to slow down after the first few tire-singing miles of the chase, he can't be sure. The car ahead grows in size, looms in the clear space of his windshield, and he knows for sure he is going to overtake and pass it in a minute or so. It is just then that he remembers to turn on the pulsing red light and touch the switch on the panel that sets his siren howling.

After that, the other car slows down in a hurry and pulls over to the side of the road. He noses in close past it, cutting sharp across and braking hard in a screech and a shallow surf of dust on the shoulder. He climbs out and now the driver of the other car is out too, a big man in a dark suit shouting something at him and clawing inside his coat below his left shoulder with a frantic hand. Larry Berlin already walking toward him sees the sudden glint of gun metal and without breaking stride he draws his own pistol from his holster and fires. By the time his finger squeezes off a second round, the big man has staggered blindly, pitched, and fallen headlong on the highway as if struck down, smashed in a broken whimpering heap by the huge indifferent fist of a giant. Larry Berlin takes a few more steps and stands over the loose-jointed, crumpled form. The man is dead. He stands there, breathing deep, profoundly astonished, looking past the shiny tips of his own boots at the dead man and the thick smear of blood slowly spreading on the road. He does not recall hearing the sound of his pistol firing, so pure was his concentration. But now he does hear something—a sigh, a rustle of clothing, or a sudden intake of breath in that breathless moment. He whirls toward the car.

Sheriff Jack Riddle is jolted out of sleep by the jangling of the phone. He knows, wide-awake but with his eyes tight closed from the first ring, that it is not the alarm clock or the doorbell or any other of the irrelevant buzzings and ringings that mark and measure a man's time. Even so, he lets it ring and ring. In the hazy false dawn between sleeping and waking, he allows himself the immense luxury of simply ignoring it a while, then speculating on what or who in the hell it might be at this hour before, exasperated, he finally rolls over heavy with a kind of a twitch and a flop like a catfish in the bottom of a rowboat. Grabs blind for the phone. Misses! It falls with a dull clatter. He wonders if he has broken it, but it rings again. Eyes still shut tight, he starts feeling for it, his right hand moving tip-fingered across a rough piece of rug and then on the slick floor until at last he blunders against the cold insistent shape.

He groans a little and lifts it to his ear.

"Yeah?"

"Hello, Jack, this is Larry."

"Okay."

"I just had some trouble out on 27. I'm bringing in a prisoner. I think maybe you better be there."

"That's what you think, huh?" he says irritably. "Meet me at the office."

He leans far over the edge of the bed to hang up the phone. He leaves it on the floor. Then he lies back on his pillow, slowly and gently as if his head were fragile as a bird's egg, opens his eyes and looks with wonder and interest at the familiar spots and cracks in the ceiling.

His wife, Betty, has not even stirred. She is sound asleep, her back turned to him, hugging her pillow like a teddy bear. He smiles. Then he eases out of bed, quiet and careful so as not to wake her, gropes on the bedside table where the phone had been, finds and lights a cigarette. He stumbles barefoot, stiff, huge and awkward as a bear on hind legs, to the bathroom. Splashes cold water on his face and, dripping, takes a skeptical look at himself in the mirror.

He is a big man, big-boned and heavy, with a large, round, close-cropped head, cut so close to the scalp that the patches of gray are like a light stain. He likes it cut that way. Keeps him from having to think about it. When he was a boy, he was called Cannonball because of that head. His eyes are greenish in the light like a cat's and fringed with pale, sparse lashes. His nose is broad and flat and broken. He has a hard, sunburned face, cut with the fine deep lines of wind and open weather. But for all the intrinsic sculptured strength and brutality, it is a warm face. He is quick to smile and at ease with his power. He runs his fingers across his bristly cheek. He won't take the time to shave and have breakfast with Betty.

Yesterday's khaki uniform is in a rumpled pile on a

chair. He might as well wait until later to change his clothes, too. He slips into the khakis, kneels to lace and tie his high-top shoes, and leaves the bedroom and the small frame house, pausing at the door to pick up his gray, battered, broad-brimmed hat. Pulls the front door to softly behind him. Squares his hat, hikes his britches and steps over the rolled-up paper on the stoop, figuring he can save that for later, too. Climbs in his car, easing his bulk behind the wheel, allows himself a long sigh, then starts the engine and backs out of the driveway.

The town of Fairview is small and old. It is the county seat. It offers for casual inspection a wide main street flanked by low brick buildings and running into and then out of a shady green park where the county courthouse stands and behind that, hidden from view, the squat two-storied shape of the county jail. The highway races headlong into Fairview from pine woods and miles of bright, bare, flat fields, snarls up and passes slowly for a few minutes through the dense, pleasant shade of the town, passes by the brick buildings, the brief glitter of store fronts and sidewalks, ducks under more shade trees, going by wide lawns now and white frame houses set back at a comfortable, old-fashioned distance from the street, houses grotesquely lively with the jigsawed scrolls and curlicues and latticework and even the stained glass a generation of grandparents loved. Wide, airy front porches with railings and swings and potted plants. In the yards azalea, oleander, live oak, and the inevitable rich magnolia. And then the road is gone again sprinting off breathless into the shadeless glare that leaps toward a vague horizon.

A traveler or tourist will remember Fairview, if at all, for its brief and unexpected blessing of shade and its couple of lazy traffic lights designed evidently to arrest the enormous and irresistible lunge of his progress elsewhere. He will recall it as a quiet place, a museum piece from the past, where he was forced to sit with foot-tapping impatience waiting for a light to turn from red to green.

Fairview is anachronistic, dying, but endures still as the center and hub of a sprawling, lightly populated county given over to small farming, ranching, and a few logging and turpentine camps. Before the turn of the century there was a short, deceptive period of prosperity, a fatness from the profits of naval stores. Most of the brick buildings and most of the big, fine houses were built on those profits. And, again, just before the Depression gripped the amazed nation in an iron fist, there was a time for a fantastic, gaudy daydream based upon a wildly inflated notion of the value of the raw land of the peninsula of Florida. But Fairview, inland, lacking everything to please the tourist except a mild climate, failed early in the boom. Since then, there has been small reason for Fairview's existence, except as a place for the people already there to age and die in, except as the legal and material heart of a poor rural county. Except as a place with a few commonplace memories and the dusty official archives. The town endures now in the affluent middle of the century without thriving and without really changing much, a preserved relic, it seems, of what at least from this anxious point in human history was an easier, gentler, more relaxed time to be alive. The only recent additions to the face of the town are the Bide-A-Wee Motel on the north edge, the Winn-Dixie Supermarket, and the glass and concrete of the hospital and medical center.

"At least we can die in a new building," the natives say.

The county jail was built well before the First World War. It is brick too (there was a mayor in the brick business) and as solid as a fort or a blockhouse. It seems to have sagged at joint and sinew with age, to have hunched down on arthritic hams and settled into the earth. Or, perhaps, simply to have grown out of the earth like some monstrous plant. The long shadow of the stern, cupolaed courthouse falls across the lawn and reaches the front steps of the jail behind it. The upper story of the jail is for confinement, a row of small barred windows running completely around the building. Pass close by at certain times, like twilight, and you are likely to see fists on some of those bars, a tic-tac-toe of black and white hands against a graph of cold steel. And sometimes a lax palm waving or imploring. And sometimes music, whistling, a snatch of a song, a harmonica. And always some laughter escapes.

In the first clean washed light of a new day, bells ringing and the crowing of roosters echoing across the back fences of the town, the jail seems most shabby and forlorn. By the end of the day, light fading and one more day spent and smirched, it appears almost comfortable. This morning, as he drives up to leave his car in the parking lot behind it, it puts Sheriff Riddle in mind of an old hen, too old and too tough even for stewing, an old hen that has been roosting all night in a tree. Somewhere a tethered hound howls. Sheriff Riddle leaves his car and moves slowly across the crackling gravel and down a walk to the front door. He would not consider going in the back way.

Well, small and shabby as it is, it has always been enough, he thinks. *For drunks and bad driving and failure to pay fines and petty thievery and petty violence. About*

117

the last thing we need to waste good money on around here is a new jailhouse.

Trapped odor of disinfectant greets him when he opens the front door. And the odor of dust too, a ghostly compound and distillation subtly composed of the dust of all the years, the dust of public records and official forms, the dust of clothing and shoes going in and out of the building until the stone steps outside have been worn smooth and slick as a chewed bone. Dust that has eluded yesterday's sweeping and mopping details and will continue to escape somehow from all brushes, brooms, dust rags, and wet mops from now on down to Judgment Day when he or whoever else is burdened with the office and responsibility of County Sheriff will be relieved once and for all of all authority. The dust escapes it all and lingers. Just as the faint, palpable odor of human sweat and tears and misery is somehow able to overcome any disinfectant and invariably triumphs over all the perfumes of the world.

He walks through the quiet empty hallway and through a door of frosted glass with his name and title painted on it. Flips on the overhead light switch, for it is still shadowy in the room with bits and pieces of the dying night. Snoring greets him. Deep, steady snoring. A small man, also wearing rumpled khaki, is curled up on an army cot in the corner. A small, old, wizened man, the turnkey who is called Monk.

"Morning, Monk."

The snores stop. The little man sits up quickly, rubbing his eyes, and slips his feet into a pair of loafers.

"Morning, Sheriff. I was just resting my eyes a little."

The Sheriff snorts. "Your eyes are gonna need resting if you keep on looking at stuff like that."

Monk grins. Beneath the cot is a copy of *Playboy* opened to a pullout page revealing a dazzling expanse of healthy nudity—a young blond girl casually and ineffectually clutching an expensive bath towel, her expression one of pouting astonishment, as though the privacy of her bath were being interrupted by a vast reading public.

"It ain't mine. It's Larry's."

"Yeah? Well, he's about the right age for it."

"Never too old to think about it, Sheriff."

Monk is up now, on his feet, smoothing out, then folding the blanket on the cot. Sheriff Riddle moves to his desk and glances at the stack of papers and an open notebook there.

"Anybody new last night?"

"Couple of drunk and disorderly," Monk says. "You're early this morning, ain't you?"

Sheriff Riddle does not answer him. He moves around behind the desk, sits down and starts to straighten out the loose stack of papers. He hates to start the day with a messy desk, but his desk is always that way.

"Well, we had a real quiet night," Monk says, "peaceful and quiet."

The Sheriff bends over to read a letter. Reluctantly, he puts on his glasses. He gropes for a pencil and taps nervously as he reads.

"They brought in the Goatman."

The tapping ceases. The Sheriff shoves the letter aside, removes his glasses again, and looks up at Monk.

"Again?"

"I tell you, Sheriff, I just don't know what's the matter

with that old fella. He goes out and he gets two drinks under his belt and he's a holy terror."

"Hurt anybody?"

"Nobody but hisself. Fell down and busted his lip wide open."

"Do any damage?"

"He fell out before he had time to break anything."

"Poor sonofabitch," the Sheriff says.

"Seems like if you *knew* whiskey was your poison, you'd try and be a little bit careful."

The Sheriff stares at him. "How long you been working here?"

Monk smiles. His smile is a broad, weak, disastrous expression, an invitation to share a small furtive lifetime. "Long time, Sheriff. I been locking 'em up and turning 'em loose for a long time."

Which is true. Nobody spends more than six months at the most as an involuntary guest of the county. Nobody except Monk, who has spent the better part of a lifetime here, so stained now with the indissoluble pallor of prisons, the hangdog, obsequious, foot-shuffling caricature of the perennial prisoner, that he might stand as the type for all of them. Doing life for all of them. Gentle, harmless, he is at home here and nowhere else.

"Send him down," the Sheriff says. "Have him bring me a pot of coffee."

"Yes sir, Sheriff." Monk nods and leaves the room.

The Sheriff listens to him go across the hall and slowly up the iron stairs to the second floor, hollering to the sleeping prisoners to rise and shine. Soon there will be coughing and curses, shuffling noises vaguely overhead as they all roll out and clean up to start a new day. And soon from the kitchen in the back, the smell of bacon and coffee.

Sheriff Riddle gets up from his cluttered desk and looks around the small office. A few straight chairs, some filing cabinets, a radio set for contact with the cars—seldom used—a calendar on the wall, a heavy, old-fashioned typewriter resting for some reason on the floor in the corner. A cheap clothes hook where he hangs his hat. Bare with only the minimal necessary equipment to perform his duty. For anything extra, he must go elsewhere, to a more populous and prosperous county or to the State Police. He folds up the cot and the blanket and shoves them out of sight in a small closet already packed with cartons of old papers and documents. He opens the top file of the filing cabinet. He removes several coffee mugs and a paper sack of sugar. He gropes for some metal spoons. These things he arranges neatly on top of the filing cabinet. Seeing the magazine and shaking his head with a grin at the improbable young lady, he puts it in the top file. Then the phone is ringing.

"Sheriff Riddle speaking."

"This is Larry."

"Again? Where in the hell are you? I'm here."

"I'm out at the diner having breakfast."

"Where's your prisoner?"

"He's here, too. He's all right."

"Quit farting around and bring him in," the Sheriff says.

"I'll be right along. I just wanted you to know—"

"Listen, Larry, is it a nigger?"

"No."

"That's a blessing."

"Okay, I'll be along in a few minutes."

Sheriff Riddle hangs up. That boy, Larry, is something

else! Stopping somewhere to have breakfast. Don't let nothing ever interfere with a meal. If you got a prisoner with you, why you just handcuff him in the kitchen or to a post or something. Sometimes that boy don't act like he's got good sense. And one of these days, he is liable to wind up being sheriff of this county. If he's got the patience for it.

The door has opened so quietly that the Sheriff doesn't notice until he happens to look there that the man called the Goatman is standing just inside the office holding onto the handle of a big white coffee pot with both hands. He is a weather-beaten man in faded, ragged overalls, barefooted, dirty, unshaven, badly hung over. He smiles at the Sheriff.

"Fresh coffee, Sheriff."

"Put it over there," the Sheriff says, gesturing toward the filing cabinet. "And pour me a cup."

He picks up the letter he had been reading and puzzles over it. It is a farmer out in the county with some kind of a tax problem. He complains bitterly about taxation in an almost illegible scrawl. There isn't anything the Sheriff can do about it one way or the other, but they all write to the Sheriff because *he* is authority; in his khaki uniform with his hat and badge the government is tangible, real, solid, not some faceless, nameless filing clerk to whom they could be little more than names and numbers on a list. "Tell the High Sheriff about it. *He'll* do something." As much trouble as it is, it is not a practice that Sheriff Riddle discourages.

"They gotta feel like they can blame *somebody*," he says.

Well, in a day or so, he'll check into it.

Looking up again, he sees that the Goatman has not moved. "What you waiting on?"

"You know, Sheriff," he says, looking down at his bare feet (he would be wiggling his toes in the dirt if there was any). "You know, I'd be honored to pour you a cup of coffee. It's always an honor to serve you in any way."

"What's wrong?"

"My hands."

"What about your hands?"

"They's too trembly."

"Lemme look at your hands," the Sheriff says. "Put that pot down and hold out your hands so I can look at them."

Arms extended, palms down, the Goatman stands shyly exposing the uncontrollable twitch and tremble of his hands. He is sweating. He tries to hide behind a bland smile.

"Just look at 'em shake!" the Sheriff says. "Ain't that something? How do you suppose they got that way?"

"I was drunk last night, Sheriff. I went out and got a little drunk."

"Did, huh? Went out and got a little drunk?"

Slowly, the Goatman has lowered his arms. Unhurried, he moves to hide his hands behind his back if he can.

"Keep 'em up where I can watch!"

Pity may be possible. Sheriff Riddle is known to be a good-hearted man. The Goatman, studying his adversary, wrinkles his brow and purses his lips.

"I feel terrible," he says. "I feel like I'm going to die."

The Sheriff is smiling at him now, a bland, untroubled, unbelieving smile. "Think you might?"

"I just might this time."

"Sit down, then. Don't just stand there and die on me."

The Goatman, immensely relieved, sits down primly on one of the straight-backed chairs. He manages to sit on his hands. He sits very straight on the edge of the chair with his knees close together and watches the Sheriff, who appears to have turned his attention to another paper on the desk.

"Might be the best thing if you did die," the Sheriff says, not looking at him. "Trouble is you're too old and tough and dirty to die."

The Goatman cackles at his cue to laugh, but he continues to watch the Sheriff, wary and apprehensive. The Sheriff looks at him again and they exchange a brief smile.

"You know what I'm going to do?" the Sheriff says. "I think I'm going to let you have a cup of coffee and a cigarette."

"I'd be much obliged, Sheriff."

"On one condition."

"What would that be?"

"It ain't too much."

Now the Sheriff picks up a pencil and writes something. The Goatman bides his time.

"What you want me to do?"

"Oh," the Sheriff says. "All you got to do is stand up straight and pour your own coffee and light your own cigarette."

"My hands is kinda trembly."

"And if you spill a drop, one little drop, so help me God, I'll make you wish you never saw my ugly face before!"

"Sheriff, my *hands!*"

"Get up," the Sheriff says. "Time's wasting."

He leans far back in his creaking swivel chair to observe this. The Goatman rises very slowly, freeing his hands, but still hiding them behind his back, a picture of study and concentration. Turning to the filing cabinet, he takes up the coffee pot and with great care manages to pour himself a cup, stopping well before the coffee reaches the rim. Setting the coffee pot down gently, he grasps the hot cup in both hands and gulps.

"One hand! One hand, goddamn it!"

The Goatman jumps at the sound of his voice and sets the cup down. The Sheriff stands up and moves toward him, hulking over him. He shrinks and cringes without actually moving, but the Sheriff brushes past. He is only pouring himself a cup. He stirs it noisily with a spoon.

"How in the world are you going to smoke with both hands hanging onto the cup?"

The Goatman grins and shrugs eloquently as the Sheriff produces a pack of cigarettes and some matches. He sets them down on top of the filing cabinet.

"Light your own," he says. "One match is all you get."

Staring, almost crosseyed with hypnotic concentration at the end of his cigarette, fumbling with his matches, striking three times before the match flames, the Goatman lifts the flame to the end of his cigarette. By gripping his wrist with his free hand, he is finally able to light it, just as the flame reaches his fingers. He drops the match. He puffs quickly, deeply. Then, triumphant, he turns to face the Sheriff.

"Well, you done it," the Sheriff says.

"Yes, sir."

"Now, then, you pick up that cup with the other hand and sit down."

Again, straight-backed, chin high, eyes watery and bloodshot, tight-kneed at the edge of his chair, the Goatman sits waiting. The Sheriff sits easy on the edge of his own desk, sitting on top of loose papers. He sips his coffee and studies the Goatman with cold eyes. Then smiles at him.

"Damn if you don't look like somebody at a tea party," he says. "You ever been to a tea party?"

Now the Goatman can laugh. The first part of the old game between them is almost over. The worst part is behind them.

"You're a better man than you think you are," the Sheriff tells him.

"You're a good man, Sheriff," the Goatman says. "You talk rough and you act rough. But you're a good man."

Sheriff Riddle laughs at this. It is a common expressed opinion of him in the county. But his role, as he conceives of it, is beyond the simple boundaries of good and bad. Outside of those convenient fences, he is not even sure what these things, good and bad, these *words* mean any more. But whatever, if anything, they may mean, he knows he is not "a good man."

"Much obliged for the coffee, Sheriff."

The Sheriff grunts and nods and then they sit there sipping their coffee and thinking.

The Goatman has been trouble for Sheriff Riddle for long years. Not by violence, for the Goatman is seldom violent to anyone but himself. And not, really, for coming in and out of the jail so regularly that he almost meets himself going in the opposite direction. But by his kind of letting go, his supreme disregard of himself as he lives in the eyes of others. Or is it, maybe, exactly the opposite? It's easy enough to imagine that he too, like the Sheriff, is playing a part, has assumed a role which makes sense

126

only in a borrowed light—the eyesight of his audience. Conscious of his own singular role, the quaintly formal gestures and attitudes rigorously required of him by the public office and trust he holds, Sheriff Jack Riddle has never been quite sure about the Goatman. And probably never will be. For the Goatman, too, lives outside the neat boundaries.

He guesses, without really caring to know, though somewhere it must be a matter of public record, that they are about the same age. He has heard the story that once in another part of the state the Goatman was a jeweler, a successful one. This is the kind of legend that a town like Fairview easily and invariably imposes on the familiar stranger in its midst. But it never fails to stir the Sheriff's imagination. It is possible to divest him of his overalls, give him a haircut and a shave and a white shirt with a necktie and to picture him seated at a jeweler's bench, squinting into the mysterious intricate jeweled hearts of watches through his eyepiece or using his long fingers gracefully to cut and to engrave letters on precious metals. Entirely possible. He has more than once declined the Sheriff's invitation to talk about it.

"That was a long time ago," is all he will say.

Now he lives as a squatter on a piece of land that belongs to somebody else. He has built himself a tumbledown shack made of bits and pieces of old lumber, packing boxes and crates. And he keeps a flock of goats. He sells goats' milk and cheese for the few things he needs, and he lives to himself like a hermit. Except for those times when he goes out to a roadside honky-tonk and becoming a public buffoon drinks himself roaring and singing and staggering into an oblivion from which he is as likely as not to awaken in the county jail. He will keep coming back. In fact, Sheriff Riddle will be disappointed if, for some reason, the Goatman should suddenly bathe, shave, dress himself and assume his rightful name and place. The Sheriff is, among other things, the chosen protector of his little world, the elected hero who must go forth to battle dragons and dark knights for them all while the towns-people live quiet and secure in the vague shine of the hidden treasure—respectability. He sees himself as a lone sentry protecting the chaste virtue of those fine houses along the main street. Within may be madness, despair, rage, and the seven deadly sins guarding a captive princess, but he is concerned only with the public world. The Goatman is a fool without cap and bells, who is somehow needed to question the value of disguise and appearances. He is respectability turned inside out. *I, too, am Man,* he says. *See for yourself.*

A trapped fly sings and buzzes against a windowpane in the office, and the Sheriff drinks his coffee and speculates about these things.

"Who's looking after your goats this morning?" he asks.

"Nobody."

"Somebody's got to tend to them, don't they?"

"Yes, sir."

"You like them goats?"

"Yes, sir."

"Better than people?"

The Goatman has to laugh. "Better than some people."

Now it is not the hum of the lone fly they are hearing, but the sound of a siren, distant and vague at first but growing louder as it screams toward them through the still streets. Sheriff Riddle jumps up and goes to the window.

128

"Damn that boy," he says. "How many times do I have to tell him not to play with that thing?"

"Who is going to look after your goats while you're in here?"

"I don't know."

The siren has cut off. They have heard the car braking in the parking lot, showering gravel. Then the slamming of the doors. Now they can hear quick heavy footsteps on the sidewalk.

"If I put you up in front of the Judge, he's liable to throw the book at you."

"Yes, sir."

Footsteps in the hall outside, then the door flies open and a man comes staggering violently into the room. He is handcuffed and his face is cut and bruised. He has been shoved hard from behind. He twists around, furious, to face the young deputy, Larry Berlin, who enters the office with a smile, carrying a sack and a guitar.

"Don't push me again," the prisoner says. "Don't you touch me again!"

Larry ignores him. He drops the guitar casually in the wastebasket and puts the sack on the Sheriff's desk. The prisoner stands there, a little hunched over, fury still written on his face, and looks around the room, squinting, puzzled. He is a fat man in a cheap suit that does not fit him. He is not a young man, but it would be hard to guess his age. He is tanned and tired.

"I got a right to know what's going on around here," he says.

Sheriff Riddle looks him up and down contemptuously, as if aware of him now for the first time. "Why don't you take a seat over there and just keep quiet 'til I'm ready to talk to you?"

"I got a right!"

Larry Berlin shoves him toward a chair. The prisoner, off-balance, staggers and almost falls again.

"Leave him alone," the Sheriff says. "He heard me."

The prisoner sits down, taking his time. The Goatman has not moved from his place, nor taken his eyes off the Sheriff. Larry goes to the filing cabinet, opens the top file and finds his magazine. He leans back against the wall idly flipping the pages.

"What was I saying?"

"You were telling me all about what would happen if you was to haul me up in front of Judge Parker. He's a very religious man. He don't drink and he don't approve of those that do."

Listening to this, the prisoner begins to laugh. He hangs his head down between his knees and laughs softly and steadily. Larry glances over the top of his magazine first at the prisoner, then at the Sheriff, but the Sheriff evidently chooses to ignore the prisoner.

"You think you're still man enough to pull sixty days?"

"No, sir," the Goatman says. "The time was when I could do it standing on top of my head. But I just can't no more. It hurts my pride to admit it, but that's the God's truth."

The prisoner is still laughing to himself.

"Your *pride*?"

"Yes, sir."

Suddenly the Sheriff turns on the laughing prisoner. He moves quick and light-footed, slapping him hard across the face. The prisoner stops laughing. Then the Sheriff returns to the Goatman.

"Your pride? What kind of pride have you got?"

"Everybody's got some kind of pride, Sheriff."

"I guess you pretty nearly got shed of yours."

"Yes, sir."

Now Sheriff Riddle goes to his desk. He leans over it and begins writing something in the open notebook.

"What are you going to do with me, Sheriff?"

"I'm going to turn you loose," the Sheriff says. "I don't see why a lot of innocent goats has to suffer because you're no damn good."

A slow, sly grin changes the Goatman's face completely. He no longer appears worn and defeated. Now he seems to have a wise face, a shrewd mask, the wary, agile wit of the long-suffering and the lowly.

"You going to let me go?"

"On one condition."

"Sir?"

"Next time they bring you in here drunk, next time I personally guarantee you a ninety-day haul. And that's going to be ninety days you'll never forget, if you live through it. I ain't going to let you mope around the jailhouse leaning on a broomstick. I'm going to put you out on the road with the young men, working from sun to dark. You'll sweat until you're as dry as an old gourd."

"Sheriff?" the Goatman says, standing now.

"Ain't you gone yet? You better get out of here before I change my mind."

"Sheriff, I ain't got a dime to my name. Not a *dime*."

Sheriff Riddle glares at him. The Goatman smiles and

hangs his head. Then the Sheriff produces his wallet and gives the Goatman a folded bill.

"What in the hell do you think I am—the Community Chest?"

"Thank you, Sheriff. I'm obliged."

"Get out!"

The Goatman scuttles out of the office like a pursued clown. Through the window they can see him run across the park waving both arms and helloing the world like a madman. Free again—

"You're making a mistake, Jack," Larry says. "He'll be right back here in a week or ten days."

"Maybe," the Sheriff says. "What's the story with this one?"

"I wasn't doing anything," the prisoner says, jumping to his feet.

"I'm not speaking to you yet," the Sheriff says.

"Listen, you big sonofabitch!"

Almost wearily the Sheriff moves close enough to hit him a lazy backhand blow across the face again. He staggers, sits back on the chair and spits a little rope of blood on the floor.

"If I didn't have these handcuffs on—"

"Take 'em off him."

Larry Berlin tosses his magazine aside, takes a key and removes the handcuffs. He steps back. The prisoner rubs his wrists and wiggles his fingers. He looks up at the Sheriff, shakes his head and grins.

"It was a hot car," Larry begins.

"Put down that magazine."

"They was driving in a hot car."

"*They?*"

"The other one was doing the driving."

"Where is the other one?"

"He had a gun, Jack."

"He never had a chance," the prisoner says.

"He had a gun," the Sheriff says.

"That's right."

"He reached for a gun and you had to shoot him."

"That's right."

"He wasn't reaching for no gun," the prisoner says. "He was trying to get rid of it. The poor bastard was hollering, 'Don't shoot me!'"

"Where is he now?"

"In the hospital."

"He's dead, Sheriff, dead!" the prisoner says, laughing again. "He was stone dead before he even hit the pavement."

"Yeah, Jack. They got him on ice over there."

Sheriff Jack Riddle whistles through his teeth. He stands with his hands on his hips looking at the young deputy. Larry is a big man too, not so heavy yet, neat and crisp in his uniform, almost too neat and military for a policeman. He used to be in the M.P.'s. The Sheriff notices his shiny belt buckle, the gleam of his boots and leather belt. In yesterday's khakis the Sheriff feels strangely ineffectual alongside Larry Berlin. Larry takes out his pistol, opens the chamber and puts two empty shells on the desk.

"Two shots," he says.

"All right," the Sheriff says finally. "First thing you've got to do is get a death certificate from somebody at the hospital. Then you come on back here and make out your official report."

Larry Berlin nods.

"You got all the stuff?"

Larry Berlin dumps out the sack on the desk. It contains two wallets, a wrist watch, change, a key ring, papers and cards, a short-barreled .32 revolver and a box of shells. Sheriff Riddle picks up the revolver, opens the cylinder, then sniffs the end of the barrel.

"Any luggage?"

"Got it in the car."

"How about the other car?"

"Wrecker came and got it. It's over to Gaston's Body Works."

"Got the registration and license?"

Larry pulls a pocket-size notebook out of his back pocket. Tears out a sheet of paper and gives it to the Sheriff.

"Well, you took care of everything. You collected it all and you wrote it all down. And then you stopped off at the diner and had yourself some breakfast."

"I was hungry. I been up all night."

"This fella give you any trouble?"

"He didn't get much of a chance. I shaped him up pretty quick."

"I can see," the Sheriff says. "Did you do it before or after you put the handcuffs on him?"

The young deputy flushes with quick anger. He bangs his fist in the palm of his other hand. "Goddamn it, Jack, if I was like you—"

"Yeah?"

The two men, heavyweights, stand almost toe to toe staring into each other's eyes. The prisoner watches, incredulous. It is Larry Berlin who looks away, adjusting his hat on his head.

"I'd be dead, that's all. I could've been killed out there."

"Maybe."

"Maybe it don't matter to you. It matters to me."

"Everything matters. Everything that happens in this county matters to me," the Sheriff says softly. "If you get killed I want to be the first to know."

Larry Berlin shrugs and crosses the room. At the door, his hand on the doorknob and the door half open, he turns back one more time. "I'll never figure you out, Jack," he says.

"That's the one thing you don't have to do," the Sheriff says, "as long as you are working for me."

Then he is gone. The Sheriff seems to slump a little, as if part of his straight, head-high posture were only a response to the challenge of Larry Berlin, the challenge of youth and strength and ignorance. He turns to look at the material Larry brought in.

Who would have thought a kid like Larry could kill somebody?

He looks around the crummy office with contempt. Wouldn't you know if he was to get busted it would be in a dump like this? Way out in the country. He has seen it all before in many other places at other times. In his time he has been pushed and beaten and ignored in places where he was a stranger. And that's just about everywhere, buddybo, ain't it? He is not afraid any more. When the young punk came out of his car shooting, he thought he was gone for sure. He scrunched down under the dashboard. He knew he was gone and he could have pissed in his pants right there. But when he finally climbed out with his hands up, the young cop was so arrogant, cocky as a banty rooster, he stuffed his pistol back in the holster at the first sight of him. Daring him to make a move, just any quick move that would allow the cop to kill him right there. The young cop, the one called Larry, grinned at him, but the eyes were flat and vicious like the eyes of a mean dog crouched over a bone. It was not a bone he stood tall and proud next to, but the body of a man. He stepped slowly, one step at a time toward the cop, his hands still as high as he could get them, locked at the elbows, never once taking his eyes off the eyes of the cop.

"All right," the deputy told him. "Stick 'em out where I can put the cuffs on you."

He lowered his hands and held them straight out side by side like a sleepwalker. The handcuffs clicked tightly in place. Then he breathed easy again. Even when the deputy, suddenly breathing hard through his mouth like he had just run a foot race or something, hit him in the face and knocked him down and kicked him savagely in the ribs, through the pain he knew he was going to be all right. He wasn't going to die. And that is something to know. He expected it. After all, a man that's come close to dying and has just had to kill somebody else has got a head of steam on him.

Now he sees his good guitar, the box he has been toting with him for almost twenty years and treating like a baby, jammed down in the wastebasket. That was unnecessary. But he knows, too, you give a young guy his initiation, let him have a little practice of his strength and power, and you can't cut it off like turning a faucet. It keeps leaking awhile. He keeps bleeding inside from the wound. The prisoner cuts his eyes away quick from the wastebasket and stares at the blank wall. If they ever get an idea you care about something, then they can hurt you. The only way you can be hurt is to have them take something you care about away from you. He doesn't trust any of them and never will, not even the big one here in the room too, the Sheriff who has on sloppy clothes like maybe he's slept in them. He hates them one and all, damn their eyes, and he will as long as he lives.

"You want some coffee, boy?" the Sheriff asks him.

"Don't try and sweet-talk me."

"If you want some, help yourself."

The Sheriff now sits down behind his desk, takes up the phone and dials. The prisoner looks past him to the wall, noticing the calendar and noticing that somebody forgot to turn the page last month. A month or two don't make no difference in a place like this. The colored photo on the calendar is of the Taj Mahal. Now don't that just beat the whole world? The Sheriff probably thinks it's in Chicago.

He does not look at the Sheriff, but he listens carefully to the half of it he can hear.

"Hello, baby . . . You okay? . . . Yeah, I'm down at the office . . . I didn't want to wake you up . . . Larry got hisself in a scrape . . . Oh, he's all right, but it's a damn mess . . . I don't know . . . Go ahead and have breakfast, I'll get something when I get home . . . Okay, baby, I'll try to—'bye."

"What's the name of this here place?" he asks after a decent interval.

"Fairview, County of Coronado."

"I ain't never even been in Fairview before."

"What's your name?"

The prisoner laughs. "You'll find out soon enough."

The Sheriff paws over the wallets, papers, keys and change. He studies the papers.

"This fella you were riding with, Tony De Angelo," he says, "what were you all up to?"

"Was that his name?"

"That's what it says here."

"Then what you gotta ask me for?"

"Just checking."

"I don't know much."

The Sheriff has picked up the revolver again. He opens the cylinder and empties the shells into his hands. He sniffs the muzzle again. "I know something. This pistol has been fired recent."

"I don't know anything about that."

The prisoner grits his teeth now and sucks in a breath. What's the use? He speaks in a flat, soft, steady, outraged monotone. Like a tired recitation.

"I was hitchhiking down the road, see? Fella stopped and picked me up maybe fifteen, twenty miles down the road from here, see? And we ain't had the time to do much more than exchange the weather and the bad news before your deputy came whaling up and run us clean off the road."

"You never saw him before?"

He laughs. Goddamn it to hell, he can't keep himself from laughing any more since this morning. That's it, that's how come the young fella hit him. He must've started laughing right out there on the road. Well, it beats crying.

"It's a great big world, Sheriff. There's thousands and thousands of miles of it and all of it is outside of this crummy county."

The Sheriff's face doesn't change. He'll hit you when

he has to, but he don't have to now. Big sonofabitch would probably make a hell of a poker player. You can't tell a thing he's thinking. Even that boy, Larry, he don't have a clue. He's liable to do most anything. He may be dumb and he may be smart, but one thing, you gotta pay something to look at his cards. He don't give nothing away until he's good and ready.

"You didn't have no *idea* it was a stolen car?"

"What do you think, Sheriff? Serious. He's going to pull up alongside me and say, 'Hop in, buddybo, if you don't mind taking a ride in a hot car'?"

"That's your story."

"It's the God's truth, Sheriff."

"Can you prove it?"

There it is again, the laughter again, bubbling up inside him like fizz water. Like he had to belch or something. Maybe it's like that, another kind of puking. The way a buzzard will puke on you. He coughs and clears his throat to stop it. Laughing ain't going to do nobody no good at all.

"You ought to be a detective, Sheriff. Like on TV."

"Can you prove you didn't know the man?"

"What can I prove? Do I look like I could prove my right name?"

A pause. The Sheriff has got a bad habit of tapping on the desk with a pencil. Makes a man nervous. Just goes to show you the trouble you can get into if you take a country boy who ought to be following behind a plow or shoveling shit and make him go to school and learn how to write. He's liable to turn out to be a pencil tapper. Now he tries to listen to something else. He hears a fly bumping and buzzing against the windowpane behind him. Somehow

it's a sad sound for him like harmonica music or the cry of
a far freight train in the middle of the night.

"This fella tell you where he was going?"

"He said something about Daytona—Daytona Beach."

The Sheriff is writing it down on a piece of paper. He
holds it crudely. He holds onto the pencil tight like it was
a carving knife. Like he was going to carve Daytona Beach
in the top of his desk. He's writing it down so careful.
What's he gonna do, bottle it for posterity?

"Where were you last night?"

"I don't have to tell you nothing."

"That's correct," the Sheriff says. "Where did you spend
last night?"

It's a funny thing about this fella. He's big and strong.
He don't have to like you. But he likes hisself enough so
he ain't going to bother to hate you. It's probably a fact
this Sheriff never hated anybody in his whole life. Oh, he
can get mad. Mad with righteous indignation. But he won't
hate you. He's probably a religious man. Takes his wife
or whoever that "baby" was, his wife, to church with him
on Sunday and stands up there in the choir and sings out
with that voice filling the whole church. A voice like that
and he ought to sing.

"Nowhere," he says. "Nowhere with a name. The cold
ground was my bed last night."

That stops him up short. Whoa, boy! That raises his
eyebrows. He is staring at the prisoner. See? He *does* listen to what you have to say. And he reacts to it sometimes.
And that's a good thing to know. And now the prisoner
can feel the mood coming over him, mastering him, getting away from him and running away. He tries to fight it,
but it's no use. What's the use? He throws back his head, a

kind of a high tilt of the chin with his eyes tight closed and he opens his mouth and sings softly in a good clear tenor voice.

> Cold ground was my bed last night
> Just like the night before—

Only a phrase from an old song, two lines from a kind of blues, white man's blues. But he feels better. Even the urge to laugh is all gone. He leans forward, gripping his hands together and looks the Sheriff in the eyes, intense.

"I been laughing, Sheriff. I couldn't help myself. I come in here laughing to keep from crying. A man don't get a whole lot of choice what he's going to do in this world. I come in laughing. I seen some things in my time, Sheriff, some terrible things, I swear to God. But in all of it I ain't never seen a man shot down right smack in front of me in the broad daylight. Like he was a mad dog—"

"Where are you coming from?"

The Sheriff, he ain't what you'd call happy, overjoyed about it neither. You can tell that from the tone of his voice even if, as soon as he's talking at you, you gotta cut your eyes away and not be looking at him. You learn that the hard way. You've seen it in a dog, even a mean one, how you can stare him down. Don't let them treat you like a dog. Don't give them half a chance. And then you can still hold up your head when you walk out. If you had've seen the way his face looked, how he looked at that boy Larry when he come to find out there was a killing! But the young one's got his point too. If you was a cop, you wouldn't want to take no chances when you run a hot car off the road. Even if you didn't know it was hot then, not 'til you had done checked the license plates against the list. If you was a cop—God forbid *that*—you wouldn't want to take no chances at all. The big one though, Jack he's called, he don't carry a gun at all. At least he ain't got one on him now. No holster and no pistol belt. Probably don't believe in it. Probably fancies he don't have to. Big man like that, looks like he could yank a tree stump out the ground or pick up the back end of a automobile if you had to change a tire. Big sonofabitch and he ain't scared of a whole lot, surely *nobody*, at least nobody he's run into yet. And if you don't have a gun and everybody knows about it, then what kind of a man is going to work up the nerve to take a shot at you? It's like a spell or a charm. What if he don't kill you? What if he was to shoot and shoot and you just keep coming on like a monster or something until you could get your big hands on him and started to ripping the meat right off the bone? It ain't all that brave to try it in the first place. If you can get away with it, you got the edge on an armed man. Make a man with a weapon feel weak. The Sheriff, he ain't scared of a whole lot. But one thing, he's scared of even *thinking* about that killing out there on the highway. He don't even want to talk about it. Right or wrong, he don't care. He don't like it even a little bit.

"Where are you coming from?" he asks again, not raising his voice.

He's a patient man for a policeman. No wonder he can get hisself elected.

"I was to hell and gone from here," the prisoner answers. "Two days ago I was clear on the other side of Chattanooga, Tennessee."

"Can you prove it?"

"You keep asking me that, Sheriff."

"I was hoping maybe you spent a night in jail or something. It might help."

"*Hoping?* What the hell do you care?"

And that's a fair question. A straight one. He's got no kind of business caring. If he cares about a thing like that, *wants* it to be so, it's a bad sign about him. He's gonna get hurt iffen he don't wind up hurting somebody else first. Because, you know, a man like that has got a tough job to do. It's a dirty job and if he starts to caring one way or the other, look out everybody. Duck! Go by the book, that's the only way. Because it just ain't true that he can really care or should much about one car thief stretched out dead that he ain't never even seen and another man sitting in his office that he's only going to see this once in his lifetime. You can't care that much. You can't hope for a stranger. The Lord knows it's hard enough to give a shit about the people you're supposed to love. And he knows that too. He's lived. He's seen a few things naked in his life. What he must truly care about, even though he may not know it yet, is that boy Larry. That must really be hurting him. More than it ought to. Like he had a stake in the boy. Like he was counting on him for something. Don't count on nothing, Sheriff, and you won't get disappointed. Couldn't you take one look in those eyes and see a killer? One look and see death? Why, sure. Surely you could. And he's been looking in them eyes a long time. *And he never even saw it!* And that's what it's really all about. What hurts the Sheriff is he has looked in the boy's eyes this morning for the first time and seen it and at the same time he seen it he knew it had been there all along, the whole time, and he had never even noticed it. He missed it until it was too late. You take a man's sense of his own judgment away from him, show him for the first time that he can guess so wrong about somebody else, when his whole life depends on that strength, and it's like cutting the legs off a man. Why, the Sheriff must feel drunk now with his new knowledge! The whole world shifting and reeling around his head. Well, you was a virgin a long time, Sheriff. And ain't that a crying shame.

"Where are you headed for?"

"Where the spirit moves me and my feet can take me."

"Where's your home?"

"Where I hang my hat. If I *had* a hat—"

"What line of work are you in?"

He's tired, tired to death of it. He knows exactly where it is going, where it's all got to go. Which is nowhere.

"Why don't you just book me and print me and lock me up and forget about it?"

"I'm trying to make up my mind," the Sheriff says. "Maybe you did just happen to hitch a ride with a fella that just happened to be driving a hot car. Let's say that's so. If it is, I don't have a whole lot of business with you or time to waste on you. I'll personally drive you out in any direction as far as the county line."

The sun is up good now. Coming in through the window behind his head. Has that old fly give up yet? Or is he just resting up a while, saving his strength so as he can buzz his wings on the glass some more? Poor little old housefly, he ain't going nowhere. Ain't nobody going to personally drive *him* as far as the county line. It's getting real warm in the room. Gonna be a hot one. The Sheriff is sweating already. You can see the dark half-moons of it spreading under his arms. You'd think they'd at least have a fan or something. Probably do, but it got busted and they ain't got around to

144

fixing it yet. Or open a window maybe. He can hear the prisoners upstairs moving around and the banging of plates and cups and spoons. Maybe if he can just get out of this here sweatbox of an office, he can still get himself some hot breakfast and even stretch out a while on a mattress and take a nap before they make up their minds and run his fat ass out of the county.

"That's thoughtful of you, Sheriff," he is saying. "Considerate. I wouldn't have to lose no more time. And time is just about the only thing I got left to lose. The county here wouldn't have to waste no beans and bacon on me. And, naturally, I wouldn't be hanging around to testify at a inquest or anything like that."

That done it. Properly! The Sheriff looks mad now. Gone and got to him. See? Because he's got his pride too, plenty of it. And he don't like to have to soft-talk and tell a lie. It isn't easy for him.

"Anything you might have to say wouldn't make any difference."

"I don't think so either," he says. "It just wouldn't all be so nice and neat, if you know what I mean."

"Nobody would believe a word you said."

Now he's laughing out loud again and letting the words free. The words coming out in the room like a startled covey of flushed quail. Let 'em go. Chattering along like a jay bird: "You right, Sheriff. Oh, you so right! I know exactly how a stranger and the word of a stranger would fare in a little old dried-up country town like this one here. Even if I was somebody, a lawyer or a banker, say, or a traveling salesman, even I was Our Lord and Saviour Jesus Christ the Righteous, Who laid down His Life even for the likes of me, and I come walking down the highway this morning preaching The Living Word of God!"

Now the Sheriff laughs, surprising him. "You some kind of a preacher or what?"

"Some folks might say so, but not the preachers," he says. "Lock me up. I'm all through talking."

The Sheriff, still grinning, shakes his head, truly amazed. Then he lifts the phone off the hook and, turning slightly in the swivel chair so that he doesn't have to look at the prisoner while he's talking and so that unless the prisoner is a very good, jailhouse-trained listener, he won't hear what's being said, he dials and waits.

"Sheriff?"

"Huh?"

"What you waiting on?"

The Sheriff hangs up. He lights a cigarette. "Me? I'm just waiting for Larry to get back with that certificate."

"That might take a while."

"Maybe."

The Sheriff is dialing again.

"Sheriff?"

"Huh?" He's getting annoyed now. Messed him up in the middle of dialing and he's got to hang up and start over.

"You mind if I pick up my box out of the wastebasket?" Cutting his eyes toward the guitar and then away again quickly.

"Help yourself."

He can't help grinning to himself while the Sheriff dials again. The young one would probably bust it over his head right about now. The prisoner has been working at it, waiting to get his nervous hands on that box ever since he came

146

in. You got to sneak up on something like that. Work all around it slow and easy, that old buzzard again circling up in the sky like a piece of burnt paper, biding his sweet time. Then the time comes and you pounce. Right time comes along and you can just ask right out and get a straight answer.

He slips out of his coat and hangs it on the back of the chair. Rolls up his sleeves over fat forearms to the elbows. Then moves to lift that box tenderly out of the wastebasket. Not a new scratch on it. Which is a blessing and a wonder, the way that boy was banging it around. Runs his hands up and down the neck and the body of it. Spanish-type guitar with a good woman shape. Real good Spanish guitar a long time ago to start out with. Bought it off a blind nigger in Galveston. Shipping out then in those days, working the Gulf. Been to many a place. Mexico, Panama, Cuba. Oh, lots of places. And that box was always good company. Only seen one just like it and that was one a Cuban had in Ybor City down at Tampa and they stayed up all night playing and singing in a bar until the dawn come on and they walked back to the ship, playing and singing right down the street together and right up to the gangway and the last thing he seen was that Cuban standing all alone at the end of the wharf playing and singing while the ship pulled out. Ybor City, now that was a wild place in those days! You could see most everything. And you could eat there. All that good Spanish food, black beans and rice and chicken and all those things. Always did like Spanish people. Even the Mexicans. Been through hell and high water, flood and fire, ever since then. Got tough old steel strings on it. Like to have nylon like the good guitar players because it sounds better, though you got to learn to listen to it. Softer, but a whole lot better.

Tuning, he plucks one string very softly, with his ear right up next to the neck. He comes on down—E, B, G, D, A, E again. It's way out of tune. He fiddles with it, 'til it's tuned as right as it will be. Then he plucks one string. The little sound thrills the drab room. He takes out his pick. ("What the hell is *this?*" the deputy asked him when he searched him. "It's my pick. I use it to pick music on that 'ere box." "Well, that looks like all it's good for. You can't hurt nobody with it and you can't get nothing for it." "Can I keep it?" Magnanimous, positively *magnanimous*: "Why not?") Wishes he was good enough, or anyway learned different, so he didn't have to use it. That Cuban could play the gypsy things and you could *see* the feet stamping down hard, the skirts flaring out and the camp-fire burning and the bright eyes of the dark men in the night, even if you had never been there and never would get there either. Now he takes the guitar to him, hooking one heel over the rung of the chair, with the body of the guitar in his lap, his left hand on the frets and his right hand loosely held to pick or strum, bending his full-moon face, a face as pocked and baggy-eyed and beat up as the man in the moon, right up close to it, playing easy and soft, hardly more than a little hum in the air and his voice so soft it might be coming from a far-distant place. The Cubans has got songs. They all got music and songs. And so do we. All different, but all saying the same things, saying the same big things anyway. He plays along and sings a little country blues tune about not owning anything and not being nobody, about being all alone day after day on the open road and sleeping all alone on the cold ground

148

by night with the stars for your blanket and the hoot of an owl or a distant freight for your lullaby. It's a true song for anybody, ain't it? Because we are all alone on that lonesome road. And whether you sleep in a featherbed with a fine woman beside you or you sleep on a hard mattress in a jail, it's all the same, you sleep alone. You sleep alone and you live alone and you die alone. Nobody knows where you come from or where you're going to. And we're all strangers, the song says between the strict simple lines, here on a tossed and whirling piece of rock lost in a black sky. We're all strangers to each other and to ourselves. We don't belong nowhere. And ain't that sad. And ain't that a crying shame. But wait a minute, don't go off blowing your nose and feeling sorry for yourself. Because a sad tune makes you feel happy. And you can think about all the good things, all the good things around you that will be here long after you're gone and was here too long before your daddy looked at your mama in a certain way. You can think about trees and stars and stones and cold water and sweet milk and the sun and the song of a bird. You can't even call up all the good things there is. All you can do, the sad tune is telling you, is rejoice, rejoice for the gift of that little bright wink of light you call a lifetime. It'll be too late if you wait 'til you're old and gray to find out. Sing a sad tune and inside you something happy starts to happen like a bunch of little children playing ring-around-a-rosy right around the broken rose of your heart.

Even so, lost in his song and the exegesis of it, he's got one trained ear cocked over to the Sheriff and his conversation, half of it, with what seems to be a sergeant at the State Police Barracks. Some people say you spoil things, doing two things at once. You don't *have* to. That's something about being a human being. You can do two, three, four, a dozen things at one time. Be here, yonder and everywhere. Ybor City and the Taj Mahal in the moonlight and never even leave a room. Different from a machine that can only do one thing at a time. So he's playing and listening.

"Hello, Sergeant, this is Sheriff Jack Riddle down at Fairview . . . Fine, thanks. How you? . . . Yeah, that's how it goes . . . Listen, we picked up a hot car for you this morning. State plates Dog 71143. Registration Number 883620. Two people in it. Driver Anthony De Angelo, address Hotel Madison, Brooklyn, New York. Other one's a vagrant. Name of—Ike Toombs . . . Yeah, double o. No address . . . Yeah, we'll have prints and the rest of it for you later on this morning. Meantime give me a call if you get anything, huh? De Angelo's got eight hundred dollars in cash in his wallet and a gun . . . Right!"

The Sheriff hangs up and swivels around again. As he does, Ike Toombs puts away his pick and strikes a loud, last, minor chord with his right hand. Puts the box down, leaning it against the wall.

"Looks like you already made up your mind."

"Just checking. Routine," the Sheriff says.

"You know something? I figured I'd be out of here by now."

"You may yet."

"You was asking me about my line of work."

"That's right."

"Well," he says with a fat, soft smile. "I don't do a whole lot of anything unless I have to. Work don't agree with me, see? I tried it once. 'Course when I need a little money

—and everybody needs a little money now and then—I sing for it."

"Pass the hat?"

"I told you I don't own a hat. But that don't stop me. I strum on this little box and I sing songs. All kinds of songs. Happy, sad, funny, every kind. Sheriff, I bet I know songs you never even heard of."

"They all sound about the same to me."

"Don't that go to show you! I picked you for a singing man yourself."

And now he picks up the guitar again and plays out loud and sings out with all his voice:

> Some folks 'preciate a singing man.
> Some folks can't, but other folks can—

Stops and his hands go slack on him and his fingers feel stiff. The song dies at birth as the sound of the siren screams up the driveway toward them. The Sheriff, angry as a hornet, is up off his chair and around the desk and over to the window, looking.

"Damn if that boy don't love the sound of that siren," says Ike Toombs cheerfully.

Larry Berlin comes walking in the office wearing a great big grin, for some reason known exclusively to God and himself, waving a piece of paper. Which the Sheriff snatches out of his hand and ascertains to be the official death certificate dutifully signed, sealed and delivered. That's how it all ends up—a piece of paper for the filing cabinet. And eventually for the closet. A piece of paper to yellow in silence and neglect and dust. Dust . . . It will outlast all of them unless the old place burns up or something. And even then, in all that confusion, somebody will probably risk his neck to save it.

"Sit down and type up your report," the Sheriff says, "before you forget what happened."

Larry Berlin shakes his handsome head to say, "Jack Riddle, you're a case!" He goes around the desk and settles in the Sheriff's swivel chair. It's comfortable. He tests it, leaning back and twisting around while the Sheriff brings the typewriter from the corner and plunks it down in front of him. Larry Berlin looks at it and tests the keys, like a brand-new toy. The Sheriff fumbles around in the filing cabinet until he finds a stack of official forms he is looking for.

"What am I supposed to do with all these?" Larry asks, taking them.

"Six copies, boy. Everything serious comes in six copies. You know that."

Larry shrugs and ineptly tries to get the forms and the carbon paper lined up correctly in the typewriter.

"You want some help?"

"I got to learn sometime."

Finally gets everything in place, smiles, then rubs his hands and flexes his fingers like a concert pianist. Bending close to the machine, he begins by diffident hunt and peck to type out his report.

Ike Toombs has been watching all this with profoundly amused concentration. It's kind of like watching a monkey play the piano or something. Worth seeing once. Now he is abruptly aware that the Sheriff has already asked him the question once and is patiently repeating himself.

"You ever been busted? You ever done time?"

"I'm not denying it. You'll find out soon enough anyway."

"Maybe we could speed things up a little."

"What's the big hurry? Like I said, Sheriff, time is all I got plenty of."

The hesitant, stumbling noise of the typewriter, like a wounded insect rattling, stops. "Gimme five minutes with him, Jack."

"I'm still trying to make up my mind," the Sheriff says to Ike Toombs. Freed from the fortress of his desk he paces restlessly up and down the small room, small for the length of *his* legs, pacing, idly picking up an object here and there, examining it without interest, without even really seeing what it may be that he has in his hands, but not looking at his prisoner directly. And speaking always in a soft, controlled voice. Like he was holding something back.

"I can't remember," Ike Toombs is saying. "I mean I been in jails and jails. All kinds of jails."

"How about the big ones?"

"Sheriff, I already told you I was all through talking."

Larry stops typing again. "Jack," he says, "you just walk outside and smoke a cigarette or something. Time you get back I'll have this smart mouth telling his life story."

"You finish up that report!"

"Lock me up! Lock me up!" Ike Toombs says. "I mean, I sure do enjoy you-all's company, but I'm going to be too late for a free breakfast."

At this moment the phone on the desk starts to ring. The sound fills the room, as shocking as a scream in the night. And for an instant all three men stop and stare at the small black instrument perched there smugly on the cluttered desk. They are tense, frozen. The sound of the phone seems to each of them and all together like a lewd interruption, a coarse fluttering tongue, a Bronx cheer offered in honor of them all.

It is Larry Berlin who picks up. Listens: "Yeah, he's here—" Cupping his hand over the speaker, offering it to Sheriff Riddle, who comes to life himself now, grabbing for it. "It's for you, Jack. State Police—"

"Riddle speaking."

And there is a long pause while he listens intently. His hard face has become completely impassive again, showing nothing, revealing no emotion or feeling, though he nods gravely as though the speaker could see him and appreciate the gravity with which he is receiving the news. Ike Toombs and Larry Berlin sit still, watching him close for a sign of anything. The barely audible voice on the other end of the tense, strung line between here and somewhere else crackles in a steady, hurried rhythm.

"All right, I'll call you back," the Sheriff says. And hangs up. Gently as if the phone were a delicate vase.

And then a thing happens. He stands bowed, staring at the cold, silent phone as if he expected it to come to life again, to rise up in the room like a wild bird and shriek at him. His face changes slowly as he stares, very slowly. He begins to smile. It is an expression Ike Toombs has not guessed the Sheriff is even capable of. A slow, relieved softening of his puzzled, outraged features. All softening like wax too close to flame. As if now it all makes sense. Something has changed radically and something else has been restored to him. Something he thought he lost forever this morning has been simply returned to him by a single phone call from a stranger.

Ike Toombs grips the neck of his guitar. He feels a chill spreading over his flesh like a cold sweat. There is something about the Sheriff's smile that is like the smile of a man who has tasted evil and found that it is sweet and good to eat. The Sheriff is a different man. Ike Toombs knows now, though he cannot let himself *believe* it yet, that he will not walk out of this office a free man. He won't walk away from this one with only a few little scratches and scars.

The Sheriff has turned away from both of them. He is pouring himself a cup of coffee. Carefully he takes two spoons of sugar and with that new smile fixed on his features, as if he now wore a stiff, painted, fierce mask, he is stirring and stirring. The spoon banging against the cup makes a noise like a little bell. Finally he lifts it to his lips theatrically. He sets the cup down and lights a cigarette, inhaling deeply the first puff. Then he picks up Larry's magazine and unfolds the picture of the young blond lady with the towel. He stares at it, meditative, smoking.

Larry Berlin has long since shrugged and returned to his typing.

"Sheriff?" Ike Toombs says.

The Sheriff turns toward him and holds up the picture. "Ain't that something else?"

Ike Toombs blinks and looks at the picture. It means nothing at all and it means everything too if you think about it. Ike Toombs stares as if hypnotized. All the women he has ever known, in fact and in the rich harem of the imagination, are dancing before his eyes—whores and virgins, sluts and nuns, dark ones and light ones, skinny and fat, short and tall, without names and a few with names and once, by God, even a wife with the name

155

of Hyacinth, which is a name that sticks. Hotel rooms and boxcars, and once standing up in the men's room on a moving train, and barns and the old green grass hotel. And maybe he did and maybe he didn't because it all happened when he was young and strong and full of the juice of life, which dries up just when you know how to use it. The old shuddering moment of *almost knowing* another human being, as close as you can come to knowledge. And the deprivation, the doing without until you learn it's one more thing you can do without, one less link on the chain you dangle from, that link by link he's pared down to where it's short enough to tolerate. What is the Sheriff telling him? He's saying a lot of things at once like a song. But most of all he's telling him, Ike, we done got there. We got the thing down to the naked truth. And he's saying something about life. There it is. Now you see it, now you don't. Take a look because it may be your last one.

"I want to talk to you, Sheriff," he says. His voice sounds strange to him. He feels he's a ventriloquist talking through a wooden dummy.

"I thought you were all through talking."

"A man is always willing to listen to reason."

The Sheriff throws the magazine away. It flies across the room in a flutter of pages and falls to the floor near the door. The girl's expression does not change. Now she's flat on her back looking at the ceiling.

"Well, now, you just listen to this," the Sheriff says quickly. If he had fangs, they would be showing now. Ike Toombs has come into the parlor of the spider, the lair of the wolf. "Seems like whoever it was in that car knocked over a little gas station in Ocala last night. And it seems like whoever it was had to go and shoot the kid that was working in the station. A high school kid. Seems like he is about to die on us."

Larry is banging the desk drawers, opening and closing them, rummaging irritably. "I can't find a freaking eraser."

"Seems like there may have been two men in that car," the Sheriff goes on evenly. "There's an eyewitness who says he saw two men in that car."

"Sheriff, I swear at the feet of God Almighty—!"

"Jack, do you know where an eraser is?"

"Ask Monk," the Sheriff snaps at him. "Maybe he's got one."

"You never can find anything around here when you need it."

Larry Berlin gets up and goes out. His heels click as he goes. Ike Toombs is amazed. How come he didn't even notice that before? Taps on his boots, naturally. He *would* wear taps. But he never even noticed it until now. Where has he been—asleep? Has the shock numbed him out like a drug? The sound of those taps takes the heart out of him.

He rises to his feet slowly. His legs feel weak and rubbery. "You mind if I take you up on that coffee now?"

"It's cold."

"I don't care," Ike Toombs says with a little giggle. "Just as long as it's wet."

Sheriff Jack Riddle watches the man the way you might observe the undulant motions of a snake in a glass case. A fat and shabby shiftless bum with his guitar and the odor and pallor of jailhouses around him like an invisible cloak. And the softness, the sag and jiggle of his belly, the soft, white fishbelly hands, the loose jowls and the rings and rolls of it cropped up around his neck, the softness is dis-

157

gusting. Probably got titties like a woman. And a little pecker like a cigarette. All the envy and pity he first felt for him has gone. Half an hour ago, ten minutes ago even, and he might just as well have turned the fella loose. Not just to save young Larry and the Sheriff's office from a bad name, though that was something to think about. But to set him on his way again. Because with all his smart mouth and the stain of toughness (which soft or hard is nothing more than the ability or the willingness to take punishment) on him, he looked harmless. Just had the old itch in his toes and on the soles of his feet to keep moving on across the dull, settled land. Never staying anywhere for long. Always a traveler. Always living in a world where everything was just exactly what it seemed to be because that's all you ever had to know about any of it. Thus in a way childlike. Like a child for whom elves are as real as rocks on the ground.

This lack of the burden of sad knowledge is enviable to the Sheriff, who has spent most of his life in Fairview. Slowly, veil by veil, the truth has been revealed to him whether he wanted it that way or not. Even though he has chosen to live by a noble illusion. For what is Justice, he thinks, with all its elaborate machinery and ritual if not the strict preservation of the illusion of the *possible* freedom and rationality of man? And he has become, by cus tom and ceremony and long usage and experience, the protector of illusion, guardian of the secret nakedness. High priest of a veiled goddess. Obedient servant of the little, flimsy illusions of respectability and decency the townspeople live by and for. Without that, he is thinking, what do they have left to worship in a bad world? The world came through in a fast car. The world came into town in the morning paper and on the TV. Lying with a smile and killing with a kiss. The world had an Italian name and lived in a cheap hotel in Brooklyn, New York. The world passed overhead, so faint you couldn't see it, leaving a vapor trail behind. He stands between the world and them. Oh, he is all too familiar with their vices and stifled virtues. But he has remained the steadfast preserver of those secrets and their illusions. Because without them, he knows and believes, life would be unbearable.

He had envied, though, to the point of admiration, the lucky ignorance that allowed a man like this one, this Ike Toombs if that is even his right name, the freedom of almost complete indifference. Innocence, ignorance, indifference, a few songs in his head like pennies in a purse. There was a kind of purity about it. That, too, was an illusion that seemed well worth preserving.

He has been wrong this time. In his own ignorance, the supreme ignorance of believing that after a certain time and a certain number of wounds and scars a man can faithfully trust his own judgment. He has failed even in his duty. He knows that he can say *that* for Larry Berlin (about whom he has guessed wrong too), he may not have had a clue or an idea what he was doing when he did it, but when he drew his pistol and shot Anthony De Angelo, whoever *he* was or might have been, without a question, as reflexively as a trained watchdog attacks a prowler, he was right. He should have killed the both of them.

"You about made up your mind to answer some questions, huh?"

The prisoner, drinking his coffee, clears his throat and nods.

"All right, let's back up. How many times you been busted?"

"There's a lot of them. A lot of little ones."

"I can imagine," the Sheriff says. "Just give me the big ones. To the best of your recollection."

"Well, they got me one time, a long time ago, on assault with a deadly weapon. I was nothing but a fresh-faced kid then. Middle of the Depression. This guy was in plainclothes. He come running at me in the freight yard. I didn't know—"

Plainclothes hell! He looked like a bum hisself. What would you do? He come running and hollering with a big stick in his hand. That was in Meridian, Mississippi. Which was a tough town on a tramp in those days.

"What else?"

"I didn't have no way of knowing he was a railroad bull," the prisoner says with sudden vehemence and complaint.

"What else?"

"Well now, the other one, the other big one . . . It was what you'd call a kind of rape, Sheriff. What I mean is, me and the lady in question, we had a little misunderstanding."

The memory of it tickles him. He can even laugh about *that* now.

"Is that all?"

"It's about enough, ain't it?"

Indignation is in that answer. You can take away a lot, but don't take away his jail pride. He's done his time, walked in and walked out where many a man couldn't. Don't make light of his suffering and endurance. A man has little enough to comfort himself with.

160

"It's enough," the Sheriff says calmly. "Probably put you smack in the penitentiary on this felony murder."

"Oh, Jesus—"

"You don't much like jail, do you?" the Sheriff says, that hard mask with the fixed smile on his face again. "A fella like you, a bum, a drifter, a singing man. You been in and out of plenty of jails. And you tough enough to take it, too. But you never got to like it. You got to have your freedom."

"What are you trying to *do*, Sheriff? What do you want?"

The door flies open behind them and they whirl around to see Larry Berlin saunter in, smiling again, holding up for everyone to see the source of his smile, a small type-writer eraser.

"Got it."

"Jesus Christ," the prisoner says.

Ike Toombs is stunned. All his life he has been acting on the hopeful assumption that if you can just keep your hands more or less clean, if you never care too deeply or obviously about anything and therefore have nothing to be deprived of, you can lose only bits and pieces at a time. No more than time and the natural process of change and decay will deprive you anyway one way or the other and without asking your permission. It's the way of the world. He has philosophically learned to include injustice in the grand design and learned to accept it. Like rain on your head. Like a stroke of bad luck. Freed in this way, freed from the fear of loss, he has been able to live and look after himself. A wily, wary life like a small scurrying rodent with sharp teeth. Alert, agile, dodging when he can and taking it when he has to. But total loss. Loss, the ultimate blind injustice of going all this way on his aimless pilgrimage only to find that death was patiently waiting for him all the time, is hard to bear. He has propitiated. He has atoned to the greater and the lesser gods. He has lived poor and alone, offering up his unattractive body and all of the things valued in the world, in return for which he has claimed only the right to live out his time. But now, he thinks, there never was a bargain. His whole life has been the working out of an equation designed to prove that life itself is ridiculous.

This morning he has seen sudden death. Not for the first time in his life, but what a way to begin this day! He has seen himself able to cause a good man (for he has been convinced ever since he was first pushed blindly into the small room that the Sheriff is a good man and that that will be his salvation) to reveal a pure and naked cruelty. Reveal a hidden hatred, hidden even from himself. He has been able to bring that out of the Sheriff like a dentist yanking a rotten tooth. He has been forced to be witness to the undeniable truth that the young deputy is neither cruel nor vicious, but merely possessed of a mindless, visceral brutality which can even be defined as innocence. It is an innocence which makes the young deputy, who just happened to be riding along the road at the same time, the exact and perfect instrument for the working out of Ike Toomb's fate.

He would curse and shake his fist in God's face now if he could. But who has ever seen the face of God?

Still, he is not defeated yet. They haven't tried, convicted and sentenced him. He still has chances and alternatives. He has the alternative of pleading for himself. A cry of mercy may be alms enough even to satisfy the Sheriff. And it seems that the Sheriff may offer him this role.

"I'm still thinking to myself," the Sheriff says. "I can turn you loose. There's no reason in the world not to believe you. You ain't got nothing to connect you with a holdup in Ocala."

"That's right. You didn't find nothing on me. No weapons, no money—"

"Or then again, I can do my duty and lock you up. Leave it to a jury to decide what to think about your story."

"You know what a jury will think."

"You never can tell."

Ike Toombs swallows hard. There is still the alternative of Job. Accepting even this and in so doing to be freed of the last humiliation. Or he can give the Sheriff what he wants, go on and say what he wants to hear. Acting on the unlikely supposition that the Sheriff hasn't already made up his mind, is not already confirmed in his will. Hoping that he can still be fooled and deluded. If he is right, he will save his life. And if he is wrong again, he will have paid out everything for nothing.

That's what it all adds up to, he thinks. *Nothing! Well now, you can't take nothing away from nothing. I went far enough in school to know that much.*

"You're kinda God in this county, ain't you, Sheriff? You say, let this one go, he don't interest me. And you say, lock that one up cause I don't like his ugly face."

"I'll tell you the truth, I don't like your looks."

"It don't matter, Sheriff. I never did want to be a movie star."

Larry Berlin laughs out loud. "You know something, Jack? He's pretty funny."

"You're lucky you're not dead already," the Sheriff says. "You could just as well be laying there right alongside of your Brooklyn buddy in the icebox."

"I never even saw that fella before this morning," Ike Toombs says. "He had a nice friendly smile. That's all I remember."

He is remembering how it was now, coming out of the pine woods, where he slept under a kind of lean-to he rigged out of some branches, with soft, sweetsmelling pine needles for his bed. He slept good, woke once in the middle of the night because a mockingbird was singing his fool head off in the dark nearby, and fell back into a deep sleep. Woke stiff and came on out of the woods to the edge of the road while it was still nighttime and the last stars were still out and the air was full of rich woodsy smells. Using a piece of old clothesline for a string, he slung his guitar across his back and set out walking slow and easy along the shoulder of the road. Walked along a good piece, feeling the stiffness coming out of his joints and legs as he moved, felt almost young again, as he often did with a good dawn and a great stretch of open road in front of him. Walked along until that white car came and stopped for him.

He was a nice, smiley, soft-spoken fella. A big guy, but he talked soft. A Yankee, but most mannersable and polite for one. Probably a traveling salesman or something, either got up real early or been driving all night, and was lonesome for the sound of a human voice.

It don't take you too much time to make up your mind do you like somebody or not. You don't, you can't never *know* what a man you meet was like before, what kind of things he done in the past. And once he drops you out the car and leaves you by the side of the road and is gone for good, the future, his future, belongs only to him also. So what do you have to go by? He gives you a cigarette and you talk along a little bit about the weather and the road. He is sick of listening to the radio and turns it off to talk to you. He's got a real nice smile. Good teeth, and he's lucky. You know him for about half an hour maybe on the highway and the only things you got to know and judge by are good. And then here come a police car running down on you from out of nowhere. And then the man is all of a sudden different. He's clean forgot about you. All he's thinking about is running for it, outrunning the cop. All the time watching in the rear-view mirror and all the time that souped-up car is gaining. De Angelo has another little smile on his face. Maybe because he seen when it come close enough that there wasn't but one man in the car chasing them. He starts slowing down. And then just about that same time Ike Toombs looks across and sees the pistol in the shoulder holster. Thinking: *Either, I hope the Lord, he's a cop hisself, or else he's some kind of a gangster.* And there ain't a whole lot left to do but scrunch down real low in the seat and hope for nothing except that whatever happens neither one of them takes it in mind to shoot you too while they're at it. Or maybe just accidentally blow your head off.

"I don't care nothing about what kind of a smile he had," the Sheriff says.

"Yes, sir, you can sit here in this crummy office in the stinking jail and let somebody else, somebody like this young fella here, do your worrying and your dirty work for you. Let me tell you something, Sheriff. You might just as well have pulled that trigger your own self."

"People like you make me sick to my stomach."

Which is literally true. Sheriff Jack Riddle feels sick. He feels like throwing up in the wastebasket. He is thinking about the *type* of which this Ike Toombs is a single, miserable example. Without roots, without ties, without anything. They are worthless. Scum! Fungus on the tired face of the earth! They breed like maggots, feeding on dead things. Bounce aimless across the country, landing one place and another like grasshoppers. A plague of grasshoppers! Might just as well have never been born.

"What about *him?*" the prisoner says.

"Who?"

"That old drunk you turned loose when we first come in."

"He can't help himself."

"You mean you can't help him," the prisoner says. "But it don't make no difference. He needs you and you need him around."

"I don't need you around."

"Turn me loose, then," the prisoner says, laughing. "Turn me loose!" Then he is serious again, but unable to resist faintly smiling at his enemy: "He's going to keep on coming back and you're going to keep on giving him his freedom."

Dirty scum spreading across the world! Corruption! You've got all the rest of it, but then you have to come here, a quiet little old town trying to die slowly in peace. With nothing for you. Where you're not known or wanted. And you've got to bring trouble and violence and bad news with you. Like a sickness. A contagious disease. People like you ought to be purged off the face of the earth—

166

"Jack? You just going to stand around and listen to all that shit?"

"I ain't going to listen any more," the Sheriff says.

He goes to the door, yanks it open and shouts into the hall.

"Monk! You, Monk!"

"You won't have to listen to me no more," the prisoner says. "Once I go out through that door, I'm gone."

"Monk! I'm calling you!"

"They're going to put me away for good," the prisoner says.

"They might."

"For something I never done."

"It's out of my hands."

Young Larry Berlin has finally finished up filling in all the required blanks on the form. The only thing he's got left to do is to fill up the blank space labeled "Remarks," where it says you are supposed to give the details of what happened in your own words. He is feeling pretty good. Lucky and glad to be alive. Before this morning he has never fired a weapon at anyone. But he feels no remorse. After all, it's what the county gives him an expensive pistol for. It's why he has to spend so much time over on the State Police Range learning how to use it. Why in the hell would they spend money on something, give it to you, teach you how to use it, spend all that time and money, and then when the time finally came expect that you wouldn't do anything? He wasn't wearing that pistol and keeping it all clean and everything just for decoration.

He took after that car because it was speeding, breaking the law. He didn't know it was a hot one until afterwards.

He wasn't thinking about anything at all then except giving the driver of that car holy hell. Chewing him out for driving that fast and giving him a ticket. Even if it was just dawn and the road was empty. What if some farmer was to come out on the road in a tractor or a wagon? He wouldn't expect nothing to be coming at him that fast and he couldn't see good in that kind of light anyway. So he run the car down and got out. And here come the driver. Then it all happened just the way you practice for it, just like they teach you. Like on a cowboy show on the TV. Or something. The big guy is going for a gun and you don't even have to think (if he had to think he'd be pushing up daisies), you reach down and find the pistol in the holster right where it ought to be and it comes out and up in a smooth fast motion. He shot fast and well. And that was a good thing to know you could do, to count on if you ever needed it. Because if you goofed the first time, you wouldn't be around to try it twice.

It's just like hunting. Shooting a deer or a squirrel or a rabbit. And it don't make any more mess than that either. If you shoot a gun at an animal you better expect to look at some blood. And, anyway, he had seen a plenty of things on the highway, right after an accident, that looked a hell of a sight worse than that did. People call you a killer if you gun somebody, even just trying to protect yourself— and ain't that the first law of nature or something? But a man drunk behind the wheel of a car, he don't call himself a murderer just because he busts somebody like an egg on the highway.

Maybe the old bum was telling the truth. Maybe the driver was really just trying to get rid of that pistol. Throw it down on the road. Well, that was his lookout. He didn't have no business carrying it around with him in the first place. He doubts it, though. If he shot the kid over at Ocala, he wouldn't be so anxious to get rid of it.

Jack has sure bugged him this morning. Giving him a bad time about everything. Jack won't carry a gun and that's his business. He can take his chances if he wants to. This morning, though, without one on him, his luck would have run out. Maybe he knows that now. Maybe it will put the fear of the Lord in his soul. You can sit on your ass around a place like Fairview and forget about a lot of things. Everybody knows who you are. You got a name and a reputation and you probably won't need a weapon. But then when somebody comes barreling in, driving a hot car and running for his life from a robbery you don't even know about yet down the road, he's going to cut you down without stopping to ask your name, rank and serial number.

This won't hurt things for Larry around the county either. He's young and new at the job, but he can't stand in the shadow of Jack Riddle forever. And he isn't planning to. Now everybody will know he's his own man.

Jack is fit to be tied by the time Monk finally gets there. He's blinking his eyes. Probably been sacked out somewhere in an empty cell.

"Where in the hell have you been?"

Monk just grins and shrugs. One look at Jack's face and he knows better than to try and come up with some kind of excuse or story. Monk may be dumb, but he's smarter than that.

"Take this man upstairs and lock him up—solitary."

Monk nods, then tips his head for the prisoner to come along with him. The prisoner takes a step, then hesitates.

He's a sly one, all right, but he ain't feeling so good now. He turns back to face Jack. Which is what you'd have to call a mistake.

"Can I keep my box with me?"

How dumb can you get? He could have walked right out of the room with it and nothing would be said. Jack's so pissed off he wouldn't even notice. When you go out of your way to *ask* for trouble, the odds are pretty good you're going to get some.

"I don't want none of your music around here."

The stupid sonofabitch is begging him now. Honest to God. Tears in his eyes and everything.

"Lemme keep it," he says. "Please. I can't live without my music."

What do you think Jack does? Finally blows his top. Goes sky high, red in the face, foaming mad. You'd have to see it to believe it because it don't happen often. Monk's popeyed.

"Give him a comb, Monk," Larry says. "Maybe he can blow music on a comb."

You got to give it to the prisoner. Once it's gone, it's gone. He quits crying like you shut off the water valve and he slips on his coat that don't fit worth a damn and tries to suck in that belly and hold up his head. Ever see a big fat slob trying to look dignified?

"Let's go, fella," Monk says.

But the prisoner, he's waiting for something more from Jack. He shakes his head and stands there staring at Jack like Jack owed him something. Jack don't want to give him the time of day. He's all through being mad, but he's finished and done with the fella. He ain't going to stand there and let him stare at him, though.

"Anybody you want notified?"

Then the nutty old fool commences laughing again. That laugh could bug you right out of your mind if you listened to it long enough.

"Answer me!"

"Nobody worth mentioning," he says.

And then Monk takes his arm and they go out, with the prisoner holding his head up very high. Once they get outside the door he gets another laughing fit and you can hear the old fool laughing all the way up the stairs.

Jack is wandering all around the office looking at everything like he never saw it before. He stoops down and picks up the guitar and puts it in the wastebasket. He stops and looks at the calendar, cusses, and rips the page off because it's a month old. He picks up the magazine and starts to crumple that up too.

"Hey, Jack, that's my magazine."

"Take it," he says, throwing it. "Keep it out of sight. What do you leave a thing like that lying around for?"

He comes over and takes the phone and calls Betty. Won't be home right away, he says. Got a lot to do. Larry Berlin is thinking maybe if he can finish this report Jack will let him go awhile. Paul is coming on duty any minute now. No reason why he should have to hang around all morning.

Jack is over there in the closet on his hands and knees fumbling around. After a while he kind of backs out. He stands up. Got a silly grin on his face. He's got something in his hands. A beat-up old leather belt with a holster on it. He puts it on. Goes to the filing case and pulls out a pistol, checks it to see if it's loaded, and stuffs it in the holster. Can you beat that?

Then he walks over to the window. There's a fly over there buzzing against the pane. Jack cups his hand to catch him. He's quick, got very quick hands for a big man. Catches that fly and holds him in the cup of both his hands. Then he opens the window with one hand and leans out and lets the fly go.

The fresh air feels good. Takes some of the stink out of the room. It's not even the middle of the morning yet, so it's not too hot. They have the sprinklers on over by the courthouse. Greenest grass in town except for the cemetery. Jack is still leaning out the window.

"Jesus, Lord in Heaven," he says.

"What's wrong, Jack?"

He turns around. "I feel so tired," he says.

Damn if he don't look wore out this morning.

"Aw, you got a lot of mileage left."

"We got work to do, boy. We got a lot of work to do on this thing."

"Yeah, I guess so."

"I feel like an old man, old and tired—"

He tucks in his shirt and hikes up his trousers. Puts on his hat. Must be going home after all to clean up and have something to eat.

"Hey, Jack," Larry says. "How do you spell 'incident'? One *n* or two?"

"How the hell would I know?" Jack yells at him. "Look it up in the freaking dictionary."

"All right, all right, all right. I was only asking."

THE SATYR
SHALL CRY

A movie soundtrack
in various tongues and voices

The wild beasts of the desert shall also
meet with the wild beasts of the island,
and the satyr shall cry to his fellow;
the screech owl also shall rest there, and
find for herself a place of rest.

ISAIAH 34:14

ONE

Dudley Hagood, editor
of the *Paradise Springs Trumpet*,
speaks his piece

When everything is at best debatable and always doubt-ful, I can't see any sense whatsoever in choosing to ignore the facts. So here are some of the relevant facts. Such as they are.

(1) It is a fact that the various incidents herein re-counted and recorded and speculated upon did take place in and about the town of Paradise Springs, county of Quincy, state of Florida. The population of Paradise Springs is slightly under ten thousand and declining. What people would once have called a "typical small town," is now a type only of the dead and wilting stalks left on the vast cornfield (actually cotton would be more appropriate regionally, I reckon) which was once America. The said field is scheduled soon to vanish forever, probably to be covered with asphalt, and the asphalt covered with painted

arrows and parking slots, all aiming to become the biggest continuous shopping center in the history of the world. That is, unless they succeed in blowing it all up first. In which case, friends, it will be the biggest desert we have yet seen, making the Gobi and the Sahara and so forth look like piddling sand piles.

(2) It is a fact that there was, indeed, a double murder, the victims being one Alpha Weatherby, a native of Paradise Springs, born and raised here, aged twenty-four, and Dan Lee Smithers, also known as Little David, an itinerant revivalist preacher, estimated to be in his late thirties or early forties, but so small and delicate of bone and stature, so pure and high in speaking and singing voice, so unlined and unblemished of skin and complexion, that (with the aid of the proper cosmetics and costume and a gold, curly wig) he could pass for a child, a prodigy chosen by the Lord to be blessed with the gift of tongues and a healing touch.

(3) It's a fact that two people were accused of, and have been subsequently tried for and convicted of, the crime of first-degree murder, involving conspiracy to commit a felony, to wit: to rob or steal from the aforesaid Alpha Weatherby the sum of $543.77, a sum which (for reasons that are not clear and not likely to be) she herself took from the Peoples Bank and Trust Company, where she was employed as a teller.

(4) It is also a fact that these two convicted criminals are presently in custody and awaiting the eventual disposition of their cases and the outcome of separate appeals filed against the decision and verdict of the jury and the sentence of the lower court. They are: (a) Billy Papp, alias "Billygoat" and "Goathead," born twenty-two years

ago in Bessemer, Alabama, and in recent years variously employed as a short-order cook, an undertaker's assistant, a used-car salesman, a carnival barker, and, at the time of his apprehension, as General Business and Promotion Manager for Little David Enterprises, Inc. The other (b) is Geneva Laseur, born Bertha Frond, aged thirty-nine, born in Big Spring, Texas, but raised and educated into maturity in a house of ill-repute in Galveston. She later enjoyed a period of prosperity and some notoriety as a specialty dancer in various places such as New Orleans, Newark, Phoenix City, and Tijuana, Mexico. This period ended when, as a result of some glandular irregularity or radical change in body chemistry, she gained an inordinate amount of weight, fat which, evidently, no treatment or weeping, praying and fasting could control or shed from her weary frame of bones. She is said to have been the common-law wife of the aforesaid Little David. This cannot, however, be established as true or false and in any case taxes ordinary credulity if not fantasy; for Geneva stands well over six feet barefooted and weighs easily as much as many professional football players.

(5) It is a fact that no trace of the missing money has been found yet.

(6) Also, no one has been able to offer a satisfactory and rational explanation of why the victim, the aforesaid Alpha Weatherby, was both as nude as and as bald as an apple at the instant of her unfortunate demise.

(7) It is a fact that following the brief and prosperous invasion of our community by reporters, cameramen, and crowds of curious tourists, life again now goes on in Paradise Springs much as it did before these unhappy events

took place. Indeed, even gossip and speculation have faded away now, the faint echo of human voices drowned out and lost against the rising volume of noise and news of the moment. That clamor is all there is. The rest is history.

TWO

Sheriff Dave Prince

I'll tell you that was one hell of a weekend. Not just the murders, though that was bad enough and trouble enough. But I surely would like to know what the whole truth of it is. There ought to be some kind of a coherent way to put all the different things that happened together in some kind of a cause and effect relationship.

But I doubt it. I mean, even if somebody knew everything that happened (and I'm probably in as good a position as anyone to know the facts), I seriously doubt he could make much sense out of it.

Don't misunderstand me on this. I don't really believe in cause and effect. That's just an idea, a convenience which can be used in trying to describe and to understand some aspects of human relations. But to take that convenient idea and try to apply it, literally and seriously, to the unhuman universe is just plain silly. No, it's more than that. It's crazy.

Try and deal with something like subatomic physics in terms of cause and effect and you will see what I mean.

You have to understand that a whole lot else happened all at once that weekend, a lot of different things that don't seem to have any connection with the murders. That's what I mean about the inadequacy of cause and effect. There are, to my knowledge, a whole lot of unconnected events, crazy-ass stuff, that happened here in the county all at the same time. And, as I already said, they don't really seem to relate much to each other in any conventional way. But the more I think about it—and, as you can see, a lot of the time I have time to think about things— the more it all seems to be part of some weirdo pattern.

Sometimes I think about that and then I find myself thinking that maybe the pattern is the only real thing and that all of the details are, well, like interchangeable, maybe even irrelevant. You know?

Those of you who saw me on TV at the time may have been briefly surprised. I doubt you would remember me, though, if you saw me again. So much is happening so fast these days. Names, places, faces and words flash from the boob tube, brilliantly and urgently lit for a moment. Then they vanish forever as they are replaced by others. People are all the time telling you what the TV gives you, what it *has to offer*, or doesn't give you and ought to. It's a topic of conversation. But when *I* look at that squatty glowing monster in the corner of my living room, what I see is not an eye but a big fiery mouth, gobbling and gobbling with an insatiable appetite, all the time hungry. An honest-to-God man-eater! And all we get is what it belches.

But I'm not here to talk about TV. I'm really just here to explain a couple of things. The main thing, the reason I mentioned TV in the first place, is that those of you who happened to see me at the time, even if you mercifully and promptly forgot me, are bound to have been surprised. Maybe even disappointed.

An interview with a southern sheriff.

I didn't look the part, to start with. I wear a dark suit most of the time, and when I wear a hat, it's a conventional, businessman's kind of a hat, felt or straw. I stand about five-seven-and-a-half and I weigh in at a hundred and forty-five. I wear glasses for reading. I often carry an attaché case. I do tend to use the accent and the idiom of my native region, but I am fully aware (even when I violate them) of the general and basic rules of English grammar. I am cognizant of the primary rhetorical and logical principles.

It is not a matter of being a smart aleck. And it is not, as some of the visiting reporters seemed to imply, a conscious effort on my part "to upgrade the image of southern law enforcement." The plain fact of the matter is that I graduated from the university with a B.A. in history, and I had completed a year and a half of law school before circumstances, which happen to be none of your business, forced me to lower my sights and to pursue a career as a lawman rather than a lawyer. I was disappointed, to be sure. But I am neither bragging nor bitching. I am only trying to explain that I have come to learn, both the hard way and the easy way, to accept certain things as they are, including some personal disappointments. And I get along

181

better with myself, on that account, and therefore I get along better with other folks, too.

Not that I would make a case for acceptance being the beginning of wisdom. Let's just say that acceptance of things as they are tends to put some limits on folly. Fair enough?

So, anyway, I didn't look the part or act the part, much to the apparent disappointment of some of the newsmen and probably "the viewing public." I beg your pardon. Sorry about that. I can't help agreeing that it showed good sense for *one* national network (never mind which) to just give up on me. They gave up on me and went out looking for the right man.

And they sure found him in Papa McDaniels. Papa, for your information, is a somewhat moronic, but good-natured old boy who, under an interesting variety of false names, played briefly and unspectacularly at defensive tackle on the football teams of a number of institutions in the Southeastern Conference. He was, in fact, a special kind of academic bum, one who could never pass any courses but who continued in his search for higher education until he got too old, too fat, and too familiar to continue in that role. Thereupon, he, too, returned to Paradise Springs, a faded hero in search of a vocation.

He drove in the stock-car races and the demolition derbies. But he was such a bad driver that he probably couldn't buy cigarettes with any prize money he may have earned. What Papa McDaniels is really good at is auto mechanics, and we weren't doing him a favor when we hired him to look after the county vehicles.

It was no wonder, then, no real cause for local surprise, when Papa showed up on that network's news program, identified as "a spokesman for the Sheriff's office." There he was, all gotten up in a khaki uniform with a campaign hat and fancy dark glasses. And don't forget the cowboy boots and the big western pistol belt, gun and holster. I hear that he really didn't want to chew tobacco and spit for the cameras, but, as I said, Papa is a good-natured boy; and he didn't think it was worth having a fuss about. All he had to do was to stand up there in that corny costume and act natural, in addition to chewing and spitting.

I offered no objection to his good fortune at the time. I even suggested that maybe he had found himself at last. Maybe he could travel around the country serving the news media as a symbol of bad law enforcement. During periods of relative peace and quiet he could be farmed out to the TV dramatic shows.

"Aw, shit, Sheriff," he said. "You are probably just kidding me."

I guess I was.

That fate and fortune would have been better than what really happened to him, though. After the media left him high and dry to sweat out his new celebrity, Papa hung around town in his TV outfit. Most people, trying to be about half decent, humored him. They listened to him tell the same stories over and over again. Then, after a time, people decided that it was probably the best thing, if life was to go on, to avoid him. That was when Papa turned kind of sour, took to drinking and fighting. Which, while not especially laudable, was certainly understandable. And, despite his size and strength, Papa is too clumsy to inflict serious damage on anyone except himself when he is under the influence.

By unspoken, mutual consensus we let his drinking and

fighting ride. But when he painted up a private car in a crude imitation of one of my official vehicles and took to cruising the public highways, harassing and arresting people (first only those with Yankee license plates, but soon his own people, black and white, friend and foe, buddy or stranger), I had to take some action. I had to act if only, for no other reason, to prevent him from being shot down by somebody a little less good-natured than himself and his oversize corpse left as an obstruction to traffic.

Some attempt to reason with him was made. But Papa kept insisting that he was the Sheriff of this county, and no matter who we thought we were, we had no right to interfere in this way.

Presently he is resting up and cooling off at the state mental hospital in Chatahoochie. There he can be a sheriff all he wants to and no harm done. When he was shipped off, I gave him a great big badge I bought at Woolworth's. It made him so happy he almost cried.

See what I mean about the *pattern?* I mean Papa McDaniels is only a minor casualty of the events which brought Paradise Springs a moment of the national attention. But a casualty he is, nonetheless, part of the pattern.

God alone knows if poor ole Papa is an important part. I don't. . . .

THREE

Darlene Blaze

I blame the whole thing, from beginning to end, on Penrose Weatherby. And I guess I will blame him till my dying day. He knew that we couldn't go there without him, so he took advantage. It was Penrose who started all the trouble.

First of all, he just kept pestering us.

"Do they have snakes?"

Frankly, we didn't know if there were going to be snakes or not. And we couldn't care less, either. No, that's not quite right. I don't care about snakes one way or the other. They don't scare me. If you stay out of their way, they won't bother you. *She* had a thing about snakes. She used to have nightmares with snakes in them. But she was determined to go whether they had snakes or not. Once Alpha set her mind on something, there was no stopping her.

"If they don't have snakes, I ain't going," Penrose said.

I tell you I was getting flat sick and tired of that kid, even if he was her brother. Him and his silly smirk all the time and his little peach fuzz of a beard and long shaggy hair. Like he was a grownup hippie or something. Beard or no beard, Penrose is nothing but a smartass kid. He is skinny as a broomstick, and he is all nervous and jerky like a windup toy or maybe a cockroach on its back, waving its legs and trying to turn over. He makes me nervous, too.

Some people say he is a little devil. I say he is a little prick with ears.

Well, I was getting sick and tired of him, as I say, playing his games, teasing us because he had the advantage. So I tripped him and knocked him down and sat on him and made him eat grass until he promised to shut up and behave himself. But Penrose, being Penrose, quick as I let him up and he got out of reach, he took it all back. And he ran off across the park, right across the middle of the public tennis court where people were playing tennis, yelling and carrying on. He ran on to where the softball diamond is, went once around the bases (*they* were trying to play a game, too) and then took off and hid in the woods on the other side of the park.

I wasn't about to give him the satisfaction of chasing after him. Alpha wasn't either. She sat down to rest in one of the children's swings. Alpha was a tall girl, you know, but she was kind of thin and delicate. She could fit in one of those swings.

She seemed kind of sad and depressed. So I gave her a few pushes, and pretty soon she was her old self and smiling again. She stood up and started pumping. She pumped the swing so high I was afraid she would loop-the-loop and come down right on top of her head.

But she checked her swing and when it slowed down she dropped off.

"Darlene, I don't have on stitch one under this raincoat."

And she didn't either. She opened the black raincoat real fast and proved it. Then she buttoned it all the way up to the top, and pulled the belt tight around the middle and smoothed out the wrinkles.

"Sometimes I have real trouble understanding you," I said.

"It doesn't matter," she said, laughing. "I'm still a virgin."

Well, I call that a low blow, especially coming from your best and oldest friend in the whole world. Just because we have a different attitude about some things. But I wasn't about to let a cruel catty remark like that—it probably just slipped off her tongue anyway—come between friendship or stand in the way of a good time. I wouldn't stoop to that, myself.

Besides, Alpha had been acting funny about clothes and all ever since I arranged for her to get some money posing for Mr. Pressy and his book. Probably I shouldn't have done that. But Pressy wouldn't hurt a flea or do anything rude. He was always a perfect gentleman in my experience. To tell you the truth, I don't think he likes girls all that much. He just likes to take pictures of girls. Anyway, Alpha said she needed money and Mr. Pressy paid plenty. So I got her the opportunity. She didn't have to do it if she didn't want to. And it didn't seem to bother her at the time. I went with her as a chaperone, so to speak. And it didn't seem to bother her at all. But afterwards she started doing weird things like not wearing any underwear.

But to go to a tent revival meeting in a raincoat and that's all . . . well, that took the cake.

"Well," I said. "I guess you'll be cool in that hot tent."

And then we walked along over towards the woods, where we found Penrose up in a tree.

FOUR

How Penrose remembers it now

He is way up there as high as he can safely climb, out on a limb and looking down at them. They are standing right under him trying to talk him into coming down. He clears his throat to spit on them and they dance back out of range. Now he takes the tennis ball he grabbed from those people on the court and he drops it right next to them like a bomb. It bounces and they jump and cry out.

He is too high for Darlene to hit him with the ball. She throws it as hard as she can, but it falls short and sails away.

"I'm going to count to ten," Darlene yells at him. "Then I'm coming up after you."

"Start climbing."

She flutters her tongue at him, loud and rude. Then she slips off her high-heel shoes and puts them down neat and side by side at the foot of the tree. She hangs her silly hat and gloves and pocketbook and nylon stockings on a bush. She gets Alpha to unzip her in back, and she wiggles out of that tight red dress. Then she spits on her hands, rubs them together while she sizes up the tree, and begins climbing.

She is amazing in bright red underwear.

Penrose thinks: *Here comes the Whore of Babylon if I ever saw one!*

She can climb as good as anyone you can think of, and in no time at all she is, too, astraddle of the same high limb, and facing him.

He edges back beyond her reach, all the while staring at the little silver cross she is wearing around her neck.

"What you looking at, smarty?"

"Guess," he says.

"Are you ready to come on down and behave yourself?"

"What'll you give me if I do?"

"I'll give you a quarter when we get down."

"Sure, sure you will."

"Don't you trust me?"

"Not especially," he says. "I gotta have some security."

"People in hell want ice cream cones, too."

So they sit there for a while, looking at each other. She is plenty mad, he knows. And he knows that what she wants to do is to start shaking the limb until he falls off and probably breaks his neck. But she won't do that with Alpha standing there. There isn't a whole lot they can do because they want to go to the stupid revival and they can't go without him. That's the rule. She glares at him and Penrose looks at the glinting silver cross.

"Gimme that," he says, pointing.

"The cross?"

"No, the red thing."

"Well, shit . . . ," she says. But she clamps her legs tight around the limb and turns loose with her hands so she can reach back and unsnap the red bra. She slips out of it, releasing an ample richness of soft flesh, white against her tan, and tosses the bra to him.

He catches it, still staring, his mouth dry, feeling a little dizzy now. The soft red thing feels like red fire, cool red fire. . . .

"Okay, Penrose, you've seen titty. Now get your skinny ass out of this tree."

She climbs down, very quick and businesslike. He smiles to himself, then climbs down after her.

"I got a quarter coming."

"Where's my bra?"

He points up to the limb where he has tied it like a small flag. It moves in the light breeze.

She says nothing. She grits her teeth and opens her purse. She takes out a quarter and hands it to him. As he reaches to take it, she suddenly fetches him a blow with the purse, a head-ringing, sight-shattering, pin-wheeling pop that turns his legs into spaghetti and leaves him sitting on the ground.

He grins and shakes the cobwebs out of his head.

"It was worth it," he says.

FIVE

Draft of Preface by Professor Moses Katz
to THE MAGIC BOOK OF WOMAN by Martin Pressy

This gathering of extraordinary photographs of the female nude is something more than it seems. That is, it is not merely another exercise in depicting and expressing the aesthetic qualities, the "beauty" of the female form, even though many of the individual photographs are, in and of themselves, "beautiful." Nor are the bodies of young women, captured and exposed here by a gifted artist, displayed for any rhetorical purpose, for *effect*. It is true that many of the individual pictures are highly sensual and celebrate the subjects as objects of desire. But Pressy does not intend to *use* his subjects in this sense. He is certainly not interested in depicting woman as a "sex object."

Representation of reality is not his aim at all. Rather this gathering is a carefully structured exploration, the record of a spiritual odyssey. The physical is not so much used as released and freed to express the spiritual essence of eternal and ineffable Woman. The Artist, a secret sharer of the profound mysteries, the *magic* of the female, himself a creature of intuition and dark impulse, is the proper figure to explore and to exploit the dark continent which is Woman. Now that we have learned, by heart and through wounds and scars beyond counting, the follies and horrors of Western rationalism, the terrors of technology and the frigid agonies of science, now that we have come at last to realize the morbid bankruptcy of the Judeo-Christian heritage (and, as well, of the Apollonian ideals), now that we have reached the end of an historical era of blindness, it is the magicians and artists who are leading us into the new, uncharted territories of the human spirit, a spirit which has been dreaming all the while Man slept and believed his own nightmares were true.

Child of the moon, daughter of the tides, preserver of the dark and hidden gods of body and blood, it is Woman who can lead us to the recovery of ourselves. And here, in this artist's *Magic Book*, we can glimpse her, nymph or fury seen in a flash of sunlight and leaves, a view like that of Orpheus when he turned back and for one blazing moment saw Eurydice once and for all.

The Magic Book is, then, at once a prophecy and a new testament, an important document for the future. It is beyond good and evil; it is at once tragic and affirmative. Silently, these naked shapes sing the oldest songs of Eden. Motionless, in the frozen moment of the photograph, they dance on and on into the future of our deepest dreams.

These are not "models," they are priestesses celebrating the mysteries of themselves in joyous self-abandonment. Indeed, in a *literal* sense none of the young women, who

194

participated with the artist in creating this masterpiece, are "models" at all. They are real and dimensional. And they are and become utterly anonymous as they blend together in light and shadow, in old song and young dance, to become the One, the Eternal Woman, forever freed from the ravages of time. . . .

Martin Pressy is a poet and a prophet. In the end he vanishes, and even his art is a splendid sacrifice to these dancers of the darkness. But *The Magic Book* remains, brimming with light and secret laughter, a celebration of all that is true of the self.

Even as I shudder at his fate, I salute Martin Pressy, who has courageously created this work of art.

SIX

Martin Pressy

If I were to blame anyone, I suppose I should blame Moe Katz and Mother.

Actually, the whole subject is rather distasteful to me now. I was terribly upset, *strung out*, at first, as much or more by all the things that happened at the tent revival meeting as by the destruction of my car and the loss of all my material. It was a very traumatic experience, make no mistake about that. But much has changed since then, and I now see it all in a different light.

Even my losses have proved to be gains.

It is true, I was (still am) a sort of amateur commercial photographer by trade. At the time I was limiting myself almost exclusively to portraits, especially of children, and to wedding photographs. I also put together the yearbook for Lanier High School and the Baptist College. But, prior to that time, I had never done any *official* work for the county; and I had no interest in or intention of doing press photography.

To be perfectly candid, I didn't need the money. I still don't.

At that time I liked to imagine myself as an artist—with a capital A. And, like many other innocent romantics, I considered Art and Commerce to be strange and hostile bedfellows.

I only opened a studio and became casually involved in my modest sort of photography because I had to be here. I was here, here to stay for a time, after Mother suffered her stroke. One has to do *something* to pass the time. It pleased Mother to think that I had a real office, a sort of *business* I could go to, and to think that I was somehow vaguely involved in this community. She has always loved it here in Paradise Springs. She grew up here. It is the center of the universe for her.

I am not trying to sound superior. It's true, I might have preferred Paris or Rome or Tangier, some exotic and more civilized place. But my tastes don't matter that much. She is a great woman, a great lady, and she can live as fully here, even in her rocking chair, as anywhere else under the sun. And where Mother lives, there you shall find me. For as long as she lives. She is fragile physically, but she has pure fire in her spirit. She may outlast us all.

When I came back from graduate school to look after her, she was concerned that I would simply stay in the old house, tending to her needs, playing cards with her, reading to her and so forth.

"I do not wish to be a burden to you, Martin," she told me. "But, by the same token, I do not wish to be bored to death by you. You must go out into the world and see what's happening. Then you will have some interesting things to talk about in the evening."

It was her idea, and I did it to please her. Of course, she was right. She always is.

The Magic Book was a phase, a stage I had to pass through, I suppose. At the time, however, it made perfectly good sense. In a strange way.

I don't regret it, mind you. An artist has very little to be ashamed of, except, of course, the neglect of his talent.

Partly, I believe now, it was Mother's fault. Not in any *serious* way, to be sure. But her lighthearted teasing made me more vulnerable than I might have been otherwise.

When I would bring back bridal photos or the prints of some wedding I had covered as part of my job, she would look at them with great interest and ask questions about all the details—who was there, what they wore, what brand of champagne (if any, in this benighted community) was served, what music, if any was played etc.

"That's what I miss most," she said, "*weddings!*"

"Why don't you attend some of them with me, then?" I said. "I will help you. We can go together."

"I prefer to look at your beautiful pictures and to hear you talking about it. It's ever so much more amusing than the real thing. I always cried at weddings, even when I was a little girl. It's foolish, I know, an old woman's vanity, but I hope that I shall never cry in public again, except, of course, at *your* wedding, Martin. Oh, I shall cry like Hecuba, once and for all, on that happy day."

"That day may never come, Mother."

"Don't say that. Don't even *think* that. Of course, you

will marry. You will marry some fine healthy girl who will have lots of children."

"Oh, mother!"

"You will do it for me, John, so that I can be a cranky and eccentric mother-in-law and a charming grandmother."

"The only reason I would ever marry is to get you to come to the wedding and to weep copiously in front of all of Paradise Springs."

It was a game, I think; no, I *know* that if I had come home then, or if I came home today, with a blushing bride-to-be, Mother would have a superb final stroke and die on the spot. But she liked to talk about it in those days.

All of her arguments were specious. Take the family name. It is my *father's* name, and certainly she has no interest in giving *that* name the least touch of immortality. Or her *social* arguments. For example, that as the most eligible bachelor in town, I owed a debt to the community, like a young prince, by choosing one girl to be the brightest flower in the garden before they all withered into weeds and nettles from neglect and shame.

I suppose she really believed that. She did not think of it as a means of redistributing the wealth in Paradise Springs. True, we are probably the wealthiest people in this community. In that sense I imagine I could be considered highly "eligible." But I should be less than honest if I did not admit that I am not well-equipped—mentally, spiritually and, yes, physically—for the prolonged rigors of conventional domestic life. No doubt but that then (perhaps even now, for I'm not yet old) I could have found someone willing to take the risk, to make the sacrifice of marrying me and living with me . . . *and* Mother. In exchange for a certain material comfort and security. Indeed there have been, from time to time, signs and portents, even, shall we say, the preliminaries of opportunity.

But marriage, as far as I'm concerned, has always been out of the question.

It was, then, a continuing game with us. Sometimes a third party was involved—our Episcopal minister, the Reverend Lee Claxton. (Aptly named. A fruitcake that poor fellow.) For his own reasons he called upon Mother as often as possible. And she brought him into the game. He joined in eagerly, trying to please her. Together they would tease me by planning the details of the most memorable Episcopalian wedding ever held in Paradise Springs.

It is possible (why not imagine the worst?) that he may have hoped, sooner or later, to arrange for the eventual bride of Martin Pressy to be none other than his own dreadful teen-aged daughter—Verna. I was spared that fate, though he, poor man, has suffered greatly on her account.

None of this is, of course, directly pertinent except in the sense that Mother's game, all this teasing discussion, planted some careless seeds which survived, grew roots.

I began to think about women—no, *woman*, infinitely mysterious woman in all her guises and forms, more and more. My loneliness, the belated arousal of simple animal desires, began to be a sort of hair shirt for me.

Fortunately, I was able to sublimate all that, to transfer and transform it into art.

Moe Katz was responsible for inspiring that. Directly. It was, I see now, his idea, not mine; though, superb Socratic teacher that he is (when he is *sober*), he led me to imagine that I had thought of it all by myself.

Twenty years ago Katz was reputed to be a first-rate medievalist. He was a very bright, very young man with a brilliant future before him, teaching at an Ivy League university. But when I came to know him he was a (prematurely) dirty old man, at the end of the line, having run out of chances, teaching remedial composition to the empty-headed girls at Southern Baptist College. Maybe the oldest assistant professor in the business. Trying his level best to stay out of *public* trouble, to hold onto his shabby job and, with luck, to sail into retirement.

Between the halls of ivy and the decayed gentility of Southern Baptist lay a wilderness of booze, pills, bad women, and a whole lot of half-assed philosophy. I hate to put it so crudely, but that is the simple story.

But Moe Katz is a fascinating old fraud. And when I returned to Paradise Springs, he was someone to talk to; more accurately, he was someone to listen to.

We first met in the sauna bath at the new Cosmo Health Spa. I was there in my ceaseless effort to fight the tendency to fat which I have inherited from Mother. He was there fighting his continual hangover. We often ran into each other at the Cosmo and soon were friends.

Katz worked on me with his fashionable and heavy talk about the dark goddesses of pre-Christian culture, witchcraft, the occult, the female principle of the universe, the magic and mysteries of Woman etc. etc. etc.

Now it all sounds too sad and silly for words, but then I was more or less susceptible. A couple of horny guys up to no good. Well, I was looking for something to do with my skills with a camera. And it was not difficult to imagine that we had been misled in our image of God. God was much more like Mother, for example, than any *man* I had ever known.

Thus the idea for *The Magic Book* began in the sweaty confines of the sauna at the Cosmo Health Club.

For the next year or so it became a sort of obsession with me, urgent yet desperately furtive. For obvious reasons.

The greatest difficulty I faced (as you can imagine) was getting the *subjects* for my art. None of them really *wanted to*. That is, they did not volunteer (with one notable exception, to be duly noted). Indeed, each in her own way was reluctant, to say the least, requiring the most careful and subtle persuasion, one might almost say, metaphorically, *seduction*. Thus, the very act of seeking out and persuading each of these seemingly reluctant subjects, while it might seem a shamefully dishonest enterprise on one level and did, in fact, cause me some grief and guilt, was nevertheless an important experience for me. And it was to become, ironically, and in ways I could not have imagined, a significant part of my development as an artist. Psychology, empathy, sensitivity to the needs, the strengths and weaknesses of each subject, were demanded of me. Some measure of real understanding, an identification with the subject, bordering upon genuine compassion, were required, though not to the extent of inhibiting me from my purpose. From all of this—call it a "confidence game," if you insist—came a better, deeper intuitive understanding of myself and my real purposes as artist.

Which is to say that gradually, as slowly yet inexorably as if the process had been a chemical one taking place in my own studio darkroom, the outlines of my design began to take shape and form. The design had always been there, I surmised, waiting to be discovered, but I could not have dreamed it before then. Yet, through blind and perhaps commonplace impulse, out of visceral and glandular gnawings, through a rich variety of rationalized whims, I staggered, clownlike, until I literally seemed to stumble upon a design of some grandeur, a statement which, I hoped, would contain beauty and truth.

I had never given much credence to concepts of fate, predetermination, predestination etc. I had never considered Man as a puppet, created by the accidents of heredity and environment, the victim or hero of his own unconscious or some vague and vast Collective Unconscious. I thought of myself, for better or worse, as Martin Pressy, a free spirit, wide-awake and conscious, thinking and being, one who saw the dim outline of a pattern or structure and at that moment exercised freely the choice to seize upon it or reject it outright.

I was, I thought, responsible for the whole of it. And I allowed myself a certain pride of achievement even though, in an undeniable way, my chief accomplishment was merely to make a choice.

In short, I was a damn fool. But, then, it took all that and more for me to come to this much wisdom.

We learn so little and so painfully.

Item. After all that intense effort at the art of persuading reluctant subjects to co-operate (the effort itself, as indicated, an education to me), I came to understand that money would do the trick. And the only real trick was determining the price. Of course, the fact that it was all for Art, that it would all be legal and correct, and that there would be no hanky-panky on the job etc., made it easier to find suitable subjects. But (I can see it now) cash was the key.

Now I must report directly about the revival meeting and the events of that night as far as they concerned me.

The reason I went to the meeting was in the hope that I might have an opportunity to talk with Miss Alpha Weatherby. Darlene Blaze, a jolly earth-girl and one of my best subjects (no trouble persuading *her*), called me and suggested that I might be able to pick up Alpha and Darlene, following the revival, and drive them home. This would give me a chance to talk to Alpha and see if she would pose for me again.

Alpha had posed for me once, and the photographs had been exceptionally fine and suitable. Though slender, almost boyish, she conveyed an intense, fiery sort of spirituality which, it seemed, added a new and wonderful dimension to my book's design.

She posed once, but then refused to pose again. And the trouble was, you see, that the prints and negatives of her session were stolen from my studio in a burglary. I lost some money and some odds and ends of replaceable equipment, and, out of my entire files, only those prints and negatives. It didn't make any sense. Darlene assured me that it could not have been Alpha herself. I was left with the conclusion that the strange burglar had been captured by the same extraordinary qualities of the girl. This only confirmed my desire to try another session with her.

"She won't do it again. I'm sure of that," Darlene told me. "Maybe I can line up somebody else for you."

I tried to explain to her that nobody else would do. I tried to express the qualities which Alpha had as a subject, the unique spiritual dimension she could add to *The Magic Book*.

"Oh, I see!" she said. "You've really got to have a tall skinny girl."

"Well, there's a bit more involved than that. . . ."

It was Darlene's stratagem that I should go to "cover" the revival meeting photographically, that I should "happen to bump into them" and should offer them a ride home.

So I packed up all the prints and negatives and releases, the entire file of *The Magic Book* in my fireproof carrying case and locked it in the trunk of my car. I had been doing this ever since the burglary. I was just closing up the studio preparing to go out to the fairgrounds when the phone rang.

It was Debbi Langley, one of Moe's students out at the College, the only one of my subjects who had given me real trouble.

A word of explanation. Moe had suggested Debbi as a natural for the book. But when I approached her she was not only reluctant, but incensed by the very idea. Though she had a marvelous figure and even some experience in modeling, she was absolute in her refusal. So be it. Except that much later, very late at night, she telephoned the house. The first I knew of it was when Mother woke me.

"Someone," she said sternly, "a young woman who says her name is 'Gypsy,' insists on speaking to you, Martin."

"I swear I don't know anyone named Gypsy."

"Well, I think you'd better talk to her if either of us is going to get any sleep. She has already called three times and will probably keep calling until you talk to her."

It was Debbi. She sounded somewhat intoxicated. She said she wanted to pose for me now, tonight, and that this would be my one chance. Now or never . . .

In my state of mind I took this as a kind of sign, a message from the muses that could not be ignored. I agreed to come out and pick her up outside the College in a few minutes.

I hurriedly got dressed.

"Martin," Mother called. "Have you gotten some little slut into trouble?"

"Oh, God no, Mother. Believe me, everything is perfectly all right. Nothing like that. I do have to go out for a while, but I promise you everything is all right."

"Just don't catch any diseases," she called after me as I was leaving.

The whole thing was unfortunate. She would have been a fine model, really, but she was drunk (or pretending to be drunk) and all the shots I got were marred, flawed by a kind of plastic sexuality. They would have been appropriate for some second-rate man's magazine, but not for my *Magic Book*.

I am sorry to report that my own flesh failed me. She literally threw herself at me after the photo session. We lay on the couch and, despite my best intentions, I found myself making "the beast with two backs" with the young lady. (Something which had never happened with any of my other subjects, I assure you.)

It was brief enough, awkward and unsatisfactory, but the damage was done. By the time I got her back to the College, to a place where she could slip under the fence and back to her dorm in the dark, she was talking of marriage.

Evidently she was not being facetious. A series of painful phone calls followed this episode. When I made it clear that, for the best interests of the two of us, marriage was out of the question, she demanded the prints and negatives back.

I would have been glad to give them to her if she had not threatened me.

Angry myself, I reminded her that she had signed a release, accepted a check in full payment and subsequently cashed it. I told her that I had no intention of returning the prints or negatives. I suggested to her that if she continued to make phone calls and threats, I would be forced to "take some kind of action." I suggested two possibilities. One was to sell them to one of the "skin" magazines, something I could legally and ethically do. The other, perhaps less kind, was to mail them in a plain brown wrapper to the Dean of Students at the College. . . .

"You wouldn't! You wouldn't dare!"

"Oh, yes, I would," I told her. "And I will, too, unless you stop bothering me."

"That's blackmail," she said.

"Not exactly," I said. "But you can think of it that way if you want to."

Sobbing, she hung up. And I had not heard of her or from her until the night of the revival.

She began by professing great shame and apologizing for her earlier behavior.

"I was afraid I might be pregnant," she explained.

She wanted to "make it up to me in some way," to "prove we were still good friends." Couldn't we meet and talk about it?

I told her, as politely as possible, that there was really nothing to talk about, but that I would be pleased to meet her some other time. I explained that I had to "cover" the revival meeting, professionally, and could not continue the conversation at this time.

"Maybe later," she said. "At the studio . . ."

"I won't be going back to the studio tonight," I said. "Call me some other time."

"Oh, you won't be going back to the studio tonight," she said, oddly I thought. "Well, then, yes, I'll call another time."

Hung up.

Suspicious ever since that burglary, I took the prints and negatives of Debbi Langley out of the files, put them in an envelope and locked it in the trunk together with my fireproof carrying case of *Magic Book*.

Then I drove out to the fairgrounds and tried to busy myself pretending to take pictures.

In the confusion after the tent caught fire, I ran to the car. It was gone. In the place where I had left it was a large black hearse, recently decorated with crude paintings of flowers and the peace sign.

There was a scrawled note on the dashboard: "DRIVE ON, DUMMY! HELL AIN'T HALF FULL YET!"

Stunned, I ran about searching for a policeman. I found Sheriff Prince and attempted to explain. But he was not interested.

"You got film in those cameras?" he demanded.

I nodded and he seized me and propelled me towards a trailer, parked a little distance from the blazing tent.

"Do something worthwhile for once in your life," he told me. "Go in there and photograph the bodies."

Which is how Alpha Weatherby posed for me one last time, together with the body of a tiny man. Both of them nude and bald as stone. I thought I might throw up at first, but soon the simple mechanical matters of taking the pictures wholly engrossed me.

Those pictures were, in my opinion, among the best I have ever made. They had more *truth* in them than the entire lost portfolio of *The Magic Book*.

So the portfolio and the book were lost forever. So my extravagant sports car was wrecked beyond repair by persons unknown. None of that matters any more.

Now I continue with my studio—children and portraits, weddings and social events. But my real life, my real art, begins when the phone rings late at night and it is Sheriff Prince or one of his men.

"Pressy," he'll begin, "there's been a terrible accident out on U.S. 17. Can you get out there right away?"

"Sure," I say. "I'm on my way."

SEVEN

Debbi Langley

If you have to blame somebody, blame Mr. Katz.

As far as I am concerned, he is responsible for the whole thing.

I hate Mr. Katz. He has ruined my life.

I didn't intend for anything bad to happen. I just wanted to get those awful pictures back. That's all.

Well, it was worth a try.

You can blame Katz to start with, because he was the one who kept telling me all about Martin Pressy and all. I had written this theme, an *assignment*, about "My Expectations in Marriage." Well, I put it down just the way I really feel. That marriage is a whole lot more than legalized screwing. That there is a lot more to life than just screwing anyway. Screwing is fun, but so are other things.

Mr. Katz always tells us to be honest, that being honest is part of our grade. So I put it down like it really is.

211

I said that the Lord had gifted me with beauty, with a neat bod that drives men crazy, so he must have intended me to use it for something.

I said I didn't want to be just another suburban housewife. My "dream," as I put it in the theme, was to do like Jacqueline Kennedy and find me a nice, rich, older man who would appreciate me a lot more than some boy my own age. (So I was "flirting" a little with Mr. Katz. Well, he likes that. And I didn't say I wanted to marry a *professor* or anything. Anyway, I thought Mr. Katz was neat in those days.)

I said that women "of substance," the wives of wealthy and important men in the community, have a lot of power and could do a lot of good if they wanted to. But by the time they get there, they are so old and tired they don't give a shit any more (or words to that effect).

I said what was needed was *young* wives for the rich and powerful. They could keep the old guys happy real easy, and without losing any sleep over it. And they could do a lot of good work in the community.

When I went to my conference with Mr. Katz, he said he had to give me a "D-minus" on account of all the little mistakes in grammar and punctuation. But, he said, my ideas were really interesting. I wasn't doing them justice. If I worked hard, if we worked hard together, I could probably end up with a very good grade, maybe even an "A."

I thought he meant it, you know. I mean, he is already past forty and too old for serious sex or anything like that. So the thought of that never entered my mind.

When his friend, the photographer, wanted me to pose bare-ass in the altogether for him (every guy with a camera wants *that*), I naturally refused. Mr. Katz told me maybe

I was making a big mistake. He said how this guy—who wasn't all *that* old—was really rich and was looking after his old mother who was dying and all. And how lonesome he must be.

I got to thinking about it. Sometimes, when I went to town, I would go and look at their big house and think about all the stuff—silver and china and jewelry and furniture—that was in it and what it would be like to live there. I would think a lot about what it would be like to go shopping every day, knowing I could buy any pretty clothes I wanted to. How it would be to have real *respect* from salesgirls and waitresses and other underlings.

I could give scholarships in my name to the College and I would never have to take any crap from them again. I could even give an endowed chair for Mr. Katz, if I felt like it.

I could travel a lot and always go first-class.

And, of course, I would do charity work and things, too.

And we could have wonderful parties in that big old house.

And I would never have to go home again.

I kept thinking about it. And finally I set it up so that Mr. Pressy had to put up or shut up. He had to fish or cut bait. And he screwed me just like I knew he would.

But he wouldn't marry me. At least not then. Maybe he was worried about his mother.

But he wouldn't marry me and he was threatening to do something terrible with those pictures.

So I *had* to do something.

I tried to get Mr. Katz to help me. But he wasn't any help at all. He said if I wanted to marry somebody, I should marry *him*. I thought he was kidding, so I laughed.

I said I couldn't make it on the money they paid an assistant professor at Baptist.

He got mad and said he had other things going for him, never mind what, but he wasn't so bad off as I might think.

Then he implied very strongly that if I intended to make a good grade in his course and to graduate, I better start putting out for him soon and regular.

God! Everything was awful. I didn't know what to do next. But I decided that the Lord didn't give me a good mind for nothing. I would *think* my way out of my troubles.

I had to get Katz off my back. And I had to see if I couldn't get even with Pressy. All I had to do was to get back on his good side first.

Katz . . . Well, I wondered what the "other things" he had going for him, and didn't want to talk about, could be. It would have to be something "shady" or he would have bragged about it.

The only thing I knew was that he was always typing in his office and late at night in his faculty apartment. Typing and typing like a madman.

To make a long story short, I sneaked in his office and found out what he was typing—*porno!* Would you believe it? Mr. Katz was writing these sex books all the time, as fast as he could type them. They were published under other names. I have actually read some of them and they weren't too bad if you like that kind of thing—corny, you know, but pretty sexy.

Well, that's no way to get rich. He probably got less than a thou per book. But he sure wrote a lot of them.

Maybe that's what was wrong with him. Writing and typing all those dirty books gave him a dirty mind.

Anyway, I got the proof on him, and then I suckered him good. I let him think I had thought things over and wanted to see him. I got all dressed up sexy and went over to his apartment and let him think he was finally going to get his jollies. Then I lowered the bomb on the bastard.

I told him I knew what he was doing and could prove it. And he would be canned so fast it wouldn't be funny if the administration ever found out. I said I expected an "A" in his composition course. And if I got "A," *maybe* I wouldn't blow the whistle on him. That's all I would promise.

I wasn't trying to be mean or anything. Honestly. But a girl has got to protect her virtue whenever she can.

That took care of old Katz.

Or so I thought at the time. . . .

As for Mr. Pressy. Well, I only intended to *scare* him. He is a nervous, sensitive type. I thought maybe he would get the message if somebody scared him a little.

That was why I got Papa McDaniels to pretend to be a sheriff or a deputy. He always had a thing about me, a cute crush sort of, the dummy. So I led Papa McDaniels to believe that I was all hot and bothered by dumb jocks and mostly him. I allowed as how I would be eternally grateful, and would *prove* it, too, if he would do me a favor and play a little trick on this older man who was harassing me and making my life miserable and all. I made it very clear I did not want the man hurt or anything like that. Just scared good. A trick. Something like the tricks that fraternity boys pull on pledges during initiation.

Papa said he could handle that okay.

I told him I would call him when the right time came.

So when I called Mr. Pressy and found out he was going

to be at the revival meeting, I thought that might be a good time.

I called Papa and told him that the man in question would be driving a white Mercedes sports car. And it would be parked out at the fairgrounds.

I didn't tell him the name, because even if he didn't know Mr. Pressy, he would sure know the name. And then he wouldn't do it.

He said fine and dandy.

Then everything you can imagine went wrong.

I sneaked into Pressy's studio to get my pictures back. I spent almost two or three hours in there, looking through everything. I couldn't find them.

How Professor Katz got hold of them I do not know!

All I know is that he has got them, prints and negatives, too, and my signed "release" and everything. He is keeping them in a safe-deposit box at Peoples' bank.

When I found out he had them, I offered to make a deal with him.

"It looks like a Mexican standoff, Mr. Katz," I said. "As long as you've got the pictures, I can't fink on you about writing that porno for money, can I?"

He laughed right in my face. Then he explained to me how he was finished with Baptist College anyway because he had just been awarded a government grant to *study porno and write a book about it!* And wasn't that a joke? He couldn't care less who I told about his hobby.

Then he suggested a deal and not a very nice one either. He said I could earn back the negatives, one at a time, before graduation.

"But Mr. Katz!" I exclaimed. "There must be thirty or forty negatives."

216

"I expect so," he said. "I haven't counted them."

Well, I thought I would fool him by accepting his deal. An old guy like that, he would probably lose interest or die of a heart attack before the end of the semester.

But, I am ashamed and sorry to report, I was all wrong. He is as healthy as a grizzly bear. He has even quit drinking. Now he *jogs* every day. You see, I forgot he was a Jew, even if he did convert to get the job at Baptist.

Well, at least I will get my diploma on schedule.

As for Mr. Pressy's car. How could I know somebody would steal it?

Papa and his buddies didn't know that they got the wrong person—whoever it was. And they didn't intend for the car to get wrecked.

But I don't have to worry about that any more. Not with Papa off at the funny farm.

I send him a postcard once in a while.

As for Mr. Pressy, I don't care about him any more.

I have met a young Baptist preacher and I think I'll get him to marry me.

A good reputation is more important than anything.

If I had known what college was going to be like, I never would have come in the first place.

But I am not a quitter. Come June and I'll be in my cap and gown with the rest of them.

As for Mr. Katz. Maybe I really am his "inspiration" now. But I sure hope he's enjoying it while he can. Because come June, all he's going to have left are memories.

Memories and a dime will buy you a cup of coffee.

EIGHT

Billy Papp's version

Now that it has all come out in the open, I want to put down exactly what happened as far as I was concerned. I am fixing to tell the truth, the whole truth, and nothing but the truth, no fooling and so help me God.

If I told any little white lies in court during the trial, it was only in order to protect others and because, being innocent, I did not realize the gravity of the situation. I did not have the slightest idea that I would end up behind bars like this. (I guess I am lucky that the Supreme Court has outlawed the *hotseat* or I would be in it, too.) I am a born optimist who believes that every cloud has got a silver lining.

That may be one reason why I am in the mess I'm in right now.

Look here, if I was even one half as slick an operator

as they say, I wouldn't be here. I would never have been working for Little David in the first place. There wasn't no money in it to speak of, not for me, except what I could arrange to pad onto expenses. He may well have been a very spiritual man. I wouldn't know about that. One thing for damn sure, though. That Little David had a pretty fair and accurate idea of the fluctuating value of a dollar. And when he felt like it, he could add and subtract like a machine.

I was a pure fool to ever fall in with him and the rest of that bunch. Now, don't that go a long way to prove my innocence?

I don't want to go so far as to pretend I am some kind of an angel or something. I have my faults. And I would like to take the opportunity right here and now to sincerely apologize for some of the things I said to the reporters after the jury brought in the verdict. I was in a state of complete shock and not responsible for what I was saying. I know that my trial was not a "joke" and a "frame-up." No man in his right mind would ever call the Honorable Judge Spence a "halfwit" or a "dirty old man." I am especially ashamed of referring to my attorney, Mr. John Rivers, Esq., as "a drunken bum who couldn't piss in a boot, let alone try a law case." He done the best he could, all things considered. Like I said, every cloud has got a silver lining, and now that I have come to my senses, I can see that my trial was a very worthwhile and educational experience. I have learned my lesson. And I am going to prove it, too, by sticking to the facts and telling exactly what I did and saw and heard. I am not going to put down any opinions and hearsay evidence.

Let's go back to the beginning.

I left Little David and the rest of them outside of Waycross, Georgia. Me and Geneva caught the Greyhound bus and came on down to Paradise Springs a week ahead of time. That's because it takes at least a week of careful planning and arranging to build up a proper interest in the show. It is a lot tougher than it used to be. Tent revival meetings have got all kinds of strenuous competition nowadays. Most people prefer to go to drive-in theaters or watch the tube or maybe go and soak up a few beers somewhere. So you gotta get their attention. What I usually do is hit a place early, slap up a whole lot of posters around town, get acquainted and get in good with the local law and the merchants, meet folks, get around town and present the right kind of image. It's all part of the business.

The reason why I went almost every night to the White Turkey is that it is widely known to be the most high-class honky-tonk in the county, and you have got to go and be seen where the best people go. And that is the exact same reason that I would drop by and shoot a few games at the Paradise Billiards Parlor. I wasn't shooting pool for the fun of it. Some got up in court and testified as to how I was a hustler. That is not so. I can shoot a pretty good game sometimes, but those people were just sore losers. You know the kind that I mean.

Usually when I'm "advance man" I work alone. But this time Little David sent Geneva along with me, "to keep me honest," as he put it. I told him he didn't understand shit about the high cost of living and the inflation. He said he would send Geneva along then to see about all that. I replied that that was no way to reduce overhead. He answered me that it was an old saying that two can live as cheaply as one.

That was the reason that Geneva and me registered as

man and wife in the motel—to save money. There wasn't nothing between us, no kind of hanky-panky. If I was fixing to shack up with somebody, Geneva would be the absolute last on my list. No offense intended to her. It's just that I don't even think of Geneva in that way. As for why we registered as "Mr. and Mrs. Hoss Cartwright," that was not for the purpose of fooling or deceiving anyone. Who would be fooled? We had both had a few cans of beer at the last rest stop before Paradise Springs and we were feeling pretty good. Besides, we had to make up *something* and put it on the register or it wouldn't look respectable.

Well . . . I was in town for one week. I put up the posters the first day. After that I spent the daytime either keeping appointments downtown or shooting pool. And at night we would go out to the White Turkey and maybe have a few beers and mingle around.

Now, this here Penrose Weatherby, the little brother of the unfortunate dead girl, he testified that he knew me well from the poolroom. That may be so, but I did not know him from Adam. That is to say, he was just a skinny, pimply kid that was hanging around, the kind you might send out to get you some cigarettes or coffee or something. I did not pay him no mind one way or the other. And I certainly did not know his name.

I was shocked and surprised when he showed up to testify in court.

And now, before going ahead with what happened on that fateful night, I would like to clear up once and for all any misunderstandings about my relationship with Miss Darlene Blaze. I would never say anything to hurt a young lady's precious reputation. I would die with my lips sealed if I thought it would do any good. But so much has already come out in public during the trial that the only decent thing for all concerned is for me to tell the truth.

Yes, we did become acquainted at the White Turkey. As it happened, Miss Blaze was without an escort at the time, her date, by the name of Buddy Joynes, to the best of my memory and recollection, having passed out cold in the parking lot where he had gone to take a pee. I happened to be nearby, myself, for the same purpose, when he fell out. She asked me would I help her put him in the back seat of his car so he could sleep it off for a while. And I gladly did so. After that, she thanked me and offered to buy me a beer, which is how we began to become acquainted.

When we came and sat down at the table, Geneva, who was feeling no pain at the time, started being a bad mouth and a party poop. And this attitude of hers was preventing me from becoming decently acquainted with Miss Blaze. I did not know what Geneva might do or say next. I began to be worried about the public image of Little David Enterprises Inc. and what might transpire if there was a bad scene. And that is the one and only reason why I put a few drops of medicine—what the Prosecutor insisted on calling a "Mickey," but what was actually a very mild sedative—into Geneva's beer while she was off in the Ladies' Room. Shortly thereafter when she had come back to our table and killed her beer, she said she felt a little dizzy and needed to get some fresh air. And that was the last we seen of her that night.

Miss Blaze observed me when I put the stuff in Geneva's beer, and she did not utter nor register any known form of disapproval.

I was not lying when I told Miss Blaze that I was in show business. I admit that I was exaggerating when I implied that I was a *bona fide* talent scout. However, my days working with the carnival taught me how to recognize and to appreciate real talent.

I offered her the audition sincerely and I honestly thought that she took the offer in the spirit which I intended.

So I was very surprised at what she said about this on the witness stand.

I quote, *verbatim*, from the transcript.

MR. RIVERS Now, then, Miss Blaze, how long did you and Mr. Papp remain at the White Turkey?

MISS BLAZE Until they threw us out.

MR. RIVERS Approximately what time was that?

MISS BLAZE Shortly after two o'clock in the morning. They stop serving at two.

MR. RIVERS And what did you do then, after, as you have said, they threw you out?

MISS BLAZE I cannot recollect too clearly. I mean there I was and I had been drinking beer pretty steady since a little after five o'clock. I guess you could say that I was a little bit high.

MR. RIVERS Do you mean drunk?

MISS BLAZE I said high. I was staggering a little but I still knew who I was.

MR. RIVERS Miss Blaze, have you ever heard of the Hitching Post Motel?

MISS BLAZE Yes, sir.

MR. RIVERS At that point, even if you were, as you say,

"high," did you feel that you were acquainted with Mr. Papp?

MISS BLAZE   More or less . . .

MR. RIVERS   Which is it—more or less?

MR. EDWARD COOK   Your honor, Mr. Rivers is justly proud of his Ivy League education and the fact that he received his law degree from fair Harvard. . . .

MR. RIVERS   Wait just a minute!

MR. COOK   But I must object to his trying to flex his expensive educational muscles for the sole purpose of browbeating this good and simple country girl. And I must object.

MR. RIVERS   And I object to counsel's insinuation that I am . . .

JUDGE SPENCE   Gentlemen!

MR. COOK   I worked my way through college.

JUDGE SPENCE   Shut up, Ed, will you please? Mr. Rivers, you may proceed with your cross-examination. But please frame your questions with more clarity.

MR. RIVERS   Thank you, Your Honor. Let's see . . .

MR. COOK   You were just getting to the good part, John. They were on the way to the motel.

JUDGE SPENCE   Order! Order in the court!

MR. RIVERS   Miss Blaze, isn't it a fact that, upon leaving the White Turkey, you and Mr. Papp did go directly to the Hitching Post Motel and that you did then proceed to spend the night with him in his motel room?

MISS BLAZE   No, sir.

MR. RIVERS   Are you denying it?

MISS BLAZE   Well, not exactly. Not all of it. Actually, see, we did not go into his motel room. He suggested that, but I refused to do so.

225

MR. RIVERS I caution you that you are under a solemn oath.

MISS BLAZE Oh, well, you probably know all about it or you wouldn't be asking anyway. It's the truth, though. I refused to enter the room that he had already bought and paid for and was living in. I insisted that Mr. Papp rent another room and he did so. We picked room 113 because 13 is my lucky number.

MR. RIVERS Why did you go into a motel room with Mr. Papp?

MISS BLAZE He was planning to give me an audition.

JUDGE SPENCE Order in the court!

MISS BLAZE He stated to me that he could help me get to the top in show business. I stated to him that I had already had a bellyful of that when I was the singer with the band at the Mickey Mouse Club before it was closed down for liquor law violations. And he stated to me that he was not talking about anything smalltime like that, or words to that effect.

MR. RIVERS Did you honestly believe that Mr. Papp intended to hold an authentic audition in room number 113 of the Hitching Post Motel?

MISS BLAZE I had my doubts.

MR. RIVERS But you went with him anyway.

MISS BLAZE I didn't have anything else to do at the time.

MR. RIVERS And did Mr. Papp actually give you an audition?

MISS BLAZE Well, we got inside and he stated to me that it was probably a little too late for a singing audition and that it would be a shame to wake up the neighbors. So we discussed the situation awhile. Then he suggested that I could do, like, a hoochy-koochy dance.

MR. RIVERS A hoochy-koochy dance?

MR. COOK They don't teach that at Harvard.

JUDGE SPENCE Shut up, Ed.

MR. RIVERS Will you, please, tell us what you mean. Explain it for the members of the jury and the others, excepting of course, counsel for the prosecution, who may not be familiar with the term.

MR. COOK Objection!

JUDGE SPENCE Listen, you two. This is a first-degree murder trial. And I would appreciate it if you would try and be serious, at least in the courtroom. You hear?

(*Counsels nod affirmatively.*)

JUDGE SPENCE You may answer, Miss Blaze.

MISS BLAZE I forgot the question.

JUDGE SPENCE He wants you to tell what a hoochy-koochy dance is.

MISS BLAZE You know, it's just that you kind of shake and dance around a little without too many clothes on.

MR. RIVERS Would you call that a legitimate audition of your talent for show business?

MISS BLAZE Well, sir, some girls can do it and some can't.

MR. RIVERS Did you execute this performance to music?

MISS BLAZE It was too late for the radio or the TV, so Mr. Papp, he put some cellophane over his pocket comb and hummed a tune through it.

MR. COOK Ask her the name of the tune, John.

JUDGE SPENCE One more time, Ed, one more smartass remark, Ed, and I'll have to hold you in contempt.

MR. RIVERS May I continue, Your Honor?

JUDGE SPENCE Suit yourself.

MR. RIVERS Well, then, after this so-called audition, why didn't you get dressed and go home?

MISS BLAZE   I figured as long as I had gone that far I might as well spend the night.

MR. RIVERS   Did you and Mr. Papp sleep together?

MISS BLAZE   There was only the one big double bed. And I wasn't about to sleep on the floor for no man.

Etc. etc. etc.

Miss Darlene Blaze made me look pretty bad in the courtroom. And everybody had some good laughs at my expense.

Mr. Rivers cleverly trapped her into admitting that she accepted a gratuity of money from me the following morning. But she even turned that around so as to prejudice my case.

He asked her if she realized that by accepting the money from me she was behaving like a common prostitute.

"Well, I am *not* a prostitute," she said. "And I have never done anything common in my whole life."

"But you asked him for money. Why?"

"I hardly knew Mr. Papp. He was new around here, a stranger in town, and I wanted to impress upon him that he couldn't take liberties with local girls just for the fun of it."

"So you were thinking of his own good and the good of the community?"

"That is correct, sir. That is exactly what I had in mind."

Well, anyway, that morning at the Hitching Post was the last time I saw Miss Blaze until the night of the revival when she suddenly showed up knocking on the door of my trailer.

It is true that I phoned her up a few times, but that was only common courtesy.

Now, then, we get to the night the murders actually took place.

Here is exactly what happened as far as I witnessed it.

We had a very big crowd show up. I had hired three off-duty Sheriff's deputies to handle the traffic and the parking and in case of any rough stuff. And also because the Sheriff, himself, had suggested it was the right thing to do. Even before the service began I paid them off, in cash and with a bonus, not so that they would leave early, but just in case they had any reason to.

I was feeling good because I could tell we were going to get a big collection. I would be up half the night counting the money. But I do not mind losing a little sleep under those circumstances.

I started to go off to my trailer, planning to settle down with a pint of vodka and an art book until the service was over.

About my art books that were seized by the police and entered in evidence against me. I have got no apologies. I am a lover of art and beauty. And I will tell you what I told the Sheriff at the time.

"If *Bunny Yeager's ABC of Figure Photography* isn't art, I will kiss your ass."

Anyway, I am on the way to the trailer when I run into this kid, that Penrose Weatherby, who is waiting for me. He says he has come all the way out here under false pretenses. He wants me to give him some money because there aren't going to be any snakes like is advertised on the poster. I explain to him patiently that it is against the law in this state to play with snakes. He states to me that if I don't give him some money quick, he's going to find a cop and claim I was trying to "molest" him.

This Penrose is some bad kid when he wants to be.

"Aren't you even a Christian, kid?"

"Don't give me that crap," he replied. "I walked all the way out here just to see the snakes you advertised."

I took a good look around. It was dark and nobody was near us. Now, I wanted to be fair to the kid. But, at the same time, I knew he needed to learn a lesson or two before he got himself into real trouble.

"Well, son, I guess you have got a point," I said, fishing in my pocket.

The greedy little runt came right up close to me with his hand out and a grin all over his face. All I did was reach out and wipe that grin off with the back of my free hand. But he fell down and rolled in the dirt and commenced hollering and carrying on. Naturally, I was concerned. If somebody came along, there could easily be a misunderstanding.

So I gave him a quarter to shut him up.

"It was an accident," I said. "I didn't mean to hit you a hard lick like that."

"Don't flatter yourself," he said. "My sister hits harder than you do."

And then he took off in the dark before I had a chance to grab him and get the quarter back.

Later, when the collection was all in, I took the money from the tent over to David's trailer. Then it occurred to me that with such a big collection—the most we had gotten in months—there might be some danger of robbery. And that is the reason I took the whole safe over to my trailer. I figured it would be safer there.

And that was the only reason I had a loaded gun with me.

About the nigger . . .

Raphael Cone has been with us for quite a while. But I would be lying if I did not admit that he can get on my nerves. When we work with a nigger crowd or else an integrated congregation, we can use him as a valuable part of the program. He has some education and he can preach if he has to. Other times, such as in Paradise Springs, he just hangs around and helps us with the equipment.

As it happens, he is supposed to keep an eye on the big crate containing the snakes.

I do not have any prejudice at all. A nigger is as good as a white man as far as I'm concerned. But I did not get along personally with Raphael. He was paid too much money, more than he deserved, because of all the things he *could* do, including to preach in a pinch. I may not have a whole lot of education in school to speak of, but I could have preached all right, too, if they had ever given me half a chance. The one time I got called upon was on short notice and that was a bad and rowdy bunch of rednecks. They were there looking for trouble and I don't think they would have listened to the Lord Himself. Nevertheless, David blamed me for the damages to the chairs and lights and tent, and he took it out of my so-called salary too.

Personally I just couldn't get along with Raphael. I will admit it was kind of silly for me to call him Rastus all the time. I would call him Mr. Rastus Coon, trying to provoke him so I would have a good excuse to whip his black ass. But that guy is some slick operator, very cool. He would keep on smiling and just ignore me. He tried to get back at me in little ways he knew would aggravate me. Like wearing those Bermuda shorts and knee socks and a pith helmet. The very sight of him strutting around in those

Bermuda shorts and that pith helmet would outrage any man. It was like he *wanted* to make me have a racial prejudice.

To top it off, sometimes he smoked with this long cigarette holder.

Well, there I was in the trailer, my trailer. I had the safe wide open and the gun in plain sight. And I was transferring the money from the safe into my suitcase because I figured that if anybody tried to rob us they might not think to look there. And *wham-bam!*, in comes Rastus Coon without knocking or anything.

"You want me to drive you, is that it?" he said.

It was my honest impression that he thought I was trying to rob the money and that he was planning to be cut in for a share. Which is why—and the only reason—I pointed my pistol at him and urged him to get the hell out of there. I had no intention of shooting anyone, not even him. But knowing that they scare easy, I thought it would save a whole lot of useless conversation.

Which it did. Because he turned around and took off running like a bigass bird.

Well, I had just about finished up transferring the money to the safety of my suitcase when in came Miss Darlene Blaze. She seemed to be all upset about something. The best I could make of what she told me was that her best friend (who later turned out to be the unfortunate Alpha Weatherby) had lost her mind in the excitement of the revival. And she had given away a lot of money that she shouldn't have, that wasn't hers.

Miss Blaze said she would do most anything to get it back.

I suggested that we could meet over at the Hitching Post later on that night and discuss the situation.

She said that would be all right with her.

I gave her a drink out of my pint and we talked a few minutes. I was only kidding with her, sort of *testing* so to speak, when I suggested that she should carry my suitcase over to the Hitching Post, for luggage, and wait for me there. A lot has been made of this suggestion on my part. But I wanted to see if Miss Blaze was really serious about her friend. I did not think that Miss Blaze would become involved in any way in what even *looked like* a crime unless she was serious and her friend was in real trouble.

But my best point was never even raised in court. Suppose, let's just pretend, I really planned on taking that money. Do you think I would have really trusted anyone to keep the suitcase for me?

There was still plenty of time before the end of the service, so I suggested to her that as long as she didn't have anything else to do, maybe she could do me another little dance like the last time.

She said she didn't have but about five minutes because she had to get back and look after her friend.

I said that five minutes was fine. I turned on the transistor radio so she could have some real music to move to this time.

"I don't know why I bother to get dressed at all," she said, jumping out of her dress and shoes and starting to dance around.

Well, with the radio playing and the air conditioner going and me concentrating on Miss Blaze's dancing, I wasn't paying any attention to what might be going on outside of the trailer. Next (and first) thing I know, Geneva Laseur comes barging into the trailer.

She takes one look at Miss Blaze and makes a wisecrack about the hot weather and ways to beat the heat.

I make some sarcasm like what did she think my trailer was—a public bus station? But Geneva wasn't interested in arguments.

"Give me your gun, quick!" she said.

"Anything wrong?"

"Let's see," she said. "The snakes got loose in the tent and the tent is on fire and David has gone crazy and is fixing to kill somebody if they don't kill him first. That's all."

And Geneva was gone.

Miss Blaze had grabbed up her clothes and vanished.

I ran after Geneva to help her, trying to do my duty in the emergency.

I do not know why I had the radio with me. I do not even remember that. I must have just grabbed it to have something in my hand.

People were running around, rushing hither and yon, yelling at each other. I was delayed getting through the crowd and the smoke. By the time I got to David's trailer Geneva was already in there and the other two were laying on the floor deader than a couple of catfish. Geneva handed me the gun back.

Then the police busted in and they didn't give anybody a chance to explain anything.

"Turn off that radio, you sonofabitch!" they told me. "You're under arrest."

Now, of course I realize that Miss Blaze sat upon the witness stand and denied outright that she ever did any kind of a dance, even a quick one, in my trailer that night.

And I realize there is no real proof that she was ever there. Except my word of honor. I don't want to contradict a lady. I try and be a gentleman and I wouldn't even mention these details if a lot didn't depend on it.

About the money . . . All I know is that it was all there, safe in my suitcase, when I left the trailer. So somebody had to take it. It wasn't me and it couldn't have been Geneva or Miss Blaze. She was out there in the dark somewhere trying to get dressed. If she had been running around in the crowd in her red underwear, she would probably have been seen and noticed by somebody.

That leaves only one other person, one person who *knew* about the money. Yes, sir, that leaves you-know-who, Mr. Rastus Coon. And I have got more than just idle suspicions. For one thing, there is the matter of the dime. A normal human being would take all of the money or, if they was in a hurry, they would probably leave some bills and change scattered around. But Rastus Coon would leave one dime behind in the suitcase for a joke.

He is a very mean one and smart, too. Remember how he acted at the trial? He showed up wearing bib overalls. And he never wore overalls before that time in his whole life. And all that "yassuh" and "no suh." Pully-wooly and "I reckon this ole shine don't rightly recollect."

The jury loved him. They actually took his word against mine.

Whoever wants to find that missing money will have to find Mr. Rastus Coon first. Just go to someplace like Paris, France, and look for a nigger in Bermuda shorts and knee socks, wearing a pith helmet and carrying a long cigarette holder. He is probably there right this minute, drinking champagne and high-price wine, screwing white women and laughing his head off.

He better laugh while he can. Because as soon as I get things straightened out, I am coming after him. And I'll find him, too, wherever he is.

I only hope he hasn't spent it all already. But you know how they are about money—here today and gone tomorrow.

NINE

Brief excerpt from the secret diary
of Penrose Weatherby

(1) Quick as we got there I slipped away. Figured they'd
never miss me. Figured correct.

(2) Saw kid switch off crazy hearse for neat Mercedes.
Left note on dashboard.

(3) Went to man (Papp) to con money. Got quarter.

(4) Walked ¼ mile to Wright's Texaco Station. Broke
one quarter. Had king-size Dr. Pepper and bag of peanuts
for supper.

(5) While there crawled under station wagon with
Yankee license plates. Loosened up radiator draincock so
it would fall out a few miles up the road in middle of
nowhere.

(6) Headed back up edge of highway towards tent.
Dropped trousers and threw moon at southbound Greyhound bus.

(7) Looking around. Hunting for snakes. Saw Papp carry small safe from one trailer to another.

(8) Found nigger sitting on crate of snakes. Told him Papp wanted him to drive him to bus station quick. Emergency.

(9) Removed crate of live snakes nigger had been sitting on.

(10) Saw nigger come busting out of trailer and run off across field. Laughed like hell. Nigger stopped running long enough to chunk rock size of golf ball and hit me with it. *Lesson to learn—when laughing at people, even in dark, keep moving.*

(11) Darlene comes out of tent, goes to Papp's trailer.

(12) Dragged crate to edge of tent. Opened it and dumped out snakes. Snakes very sluggish. Took posters. Lit some and applied fire to snakes to make more lively. Snakes crawling into tent.

(13) Peeped in Papp's trailer. Darlene doing hoochy-koochy.

(14) Tent has caught fire.

(15) Moved back into dark to observe commotion from a distance.

(16) Saw Little David run to his trailer. Peeped in. Saw Alpha there too.

(17) Rolled in dirt and ripped shirt. Crying. Ran and found cop. Said robbery going on in David's trailer.

(18) Shots. Cop ran off to trailer.

(19) Sneaked to Papp's trailer. Used shirt to hold money. Took money. Left one dime. Change from quarter Papp gave me. Good for one phone call.

(20) Also found Darlene's silver cross on floor. Took it too.

(21) Ran all the way home. Stopped in woods. Hid loot in secret place where Alpha's photographs are also stashed.

(22) Home in time to beat cops. Stuck to story.

(23) Don't have slightest idea what Alpha was trying to pull.

(24) Money safe and sound as in bank until needed.

(25) Silver cross only proof Darlene was with Papp in trailer. After trial over told her I saw her there and could prove it. Wear cross around own neck.

(26) That's all I know and all I had to do with anything.

TEN

Verna Claxton

I want everyone in the world to know that whatever my sins and faults may be or seem to be, I had positively nothing to do with anything that went on that night at Little David's Tent Revival Meeting in Paradise Springs, Florida.

The hearing concerning me and Wayne took place at a later date in the state of Arizona and it was only about things that took place within that state and nothing else.

Wayne and me were long gone, high-balling it, by the time any of that stuff took place. We were not responsible for any of it, no matter what others may say or think.

I know how people are. I know that once you have actually done one or two bad things they will lay all of the bad things that have happened on your doorstep. They think that Wayne is a terrible person. And just because I was along with him, when those things they blame on him took place, they think I am a terrible person, too.

Well, I don't care what they may think. They can think what they please. They can go right ahead thinking whatever they want to in their dirty minds.

I will simply let the record speak for itself. The whole world will take note that nothing, not a blessed thing, has ever been proved on us. We never even stood trial. If you are smart, you probably already noticed that I used the correct word, "hearing," to describe that joke in Arizona. They never tried us for anything. We were arrested and charged with stuff, that is true. And it is true that Wayne signed all kinds of statements about what we were supposed to have done. That is because, deep down, Wayne is a weakling and a coward. Naturally all that part got in the papers. But before they could even get a trial started, they had this hearing to determine if we were sane enough to stand trial. And, as you know, we both flunked. They had psychiatrists and experts and all, but none of that was necessary. They put Wayne on the stand and once he started talking, it was all over but the straitjackets. Sanity has never been one of Wayne Bixby's strong points. He is smart and he can be funny, but he is completely spaced out. That's his charm. So ten minutes after he opened his mouth at the hearing they were making space for him at the funny farm.

That is fair enough, but why did they have to put me there too? At first, I blamed it on Wayne for dragging me along with him. That was exactly what they wanted me to do. Don't you see? Well, I foxed them anyhow. I got over being mad at crazy Wayne. Then I understood the real reason I am salted away here with all these nuts. They didn't try us in court for any crimes, because they knew damn well they could not convict us. They were smart enough to figure it out for themselves that Wayne is a weakling and a lunatic. So they got him to sign all that crap. Then, before he even had a chance to change his mind, they had us both locked up in the snakepit.

The only one who could clear both of us was me. That might have given them some problems. But all they had to do was to pay off some psychiatrists to testify that I am insane too.

Naturally I reacted very strongly to their derogatory remarks at the hearing. Who wouldn't have? And don't forget I was still shocked and deeply disturbed by what Wayne had said and done there. Then Daddy, all spiffy and phony in his clerical collar, he got up there and cried and agreed with them. Daddy is so stupid and incredibly square. They probably didn't even have to pay him, not one penny for his testimony or the tears either. He flew all the way out to Arizona and back at his own expense.

Probably all they had to do was to suggest to him all the bad publicity that would come out of a real, honest-to-God court case. Daddy is terrified of his good name being hurt. So, the dirty rat, he wrapped it all up by crying and telling them I was crazy and it was all his fault and he should have put me away long ago.

Crap! Bullshit! That's what I said then, and that's what I say now.

The joke is on him because I would have been acquitted and it wouldn't have hurt his precious reputation at all.

The joke is on them too. On the dumb, crummy state of Arizona and also on the FBI, who got into the act and were hanging around because of all the alleged kidnapings and car stealings. Ho-ho-ho!

They put me and Wayne into their squirrel cage. And

they closed the books on the whole shebazz. Which is really and truly super dumb. Because if we didn't do all the things they claimed and never proved, then somebody else did, right? Weigh that, my friends. What it means is that there is still a young couple out there somewhere, knocking over gas stations and liquor stores, stealing cars, kidnaping people and giving them a bad time and sometimes even killing them. They think they are all safe now because me and Wayne are locked up.

Well, the big joke is that we are safe and they aren't. Because the real criminals are probably out there right now, barreling down some highway in a hot car, looking for kicks.

So, if that's the way they want it, they can have it. I wouldn't leave here now if they begged me to on bended knees. I just hope that that terrifying young couple comes down one more time upon the state of Arizona like a plague and I can read about it in the papers.

They will be plenty sorry then but it will be too late.

I have got the last laugh coming. All I have to do is to keep still and be patient. Why not?

But I started to tell you about that night in Paradise Springs and how we didn't have anything to do with it.

It's true I was personally acquainted with some of the people involved. That means nothing. Paradise Springs is a small town. Everybody knows everybody, practically.

Also it's true that Wayne and I were supposed to be at that revival. That's what I told Daddy. So he wouldn't worry about me.

The plan was for Wayne and me to start out for San Francisco that night. He would pick me up at the parking lot. He came wheeling up in this crazy-ass old hearse that he had ripped off of some fraternity boys in Gainesville. It was wild.

"Let's go to Frisco and do something," he said.

"Not in that heap," I told him.

"We could rip off your old man's car."

"Are you kidding? All he's got is a '51 Plymouth and it wouldn't get us to Georgia. It won't outrun a motor-scooter."

So we wandered around the lot awhile, window shopping, looking for a decent set of wheels. Pretty soon we saw Martin Pressy's white Mercedes. It was love at first sight. So we switched, leaving the hearse in its place. Nobody even saw us.

We went and had a few beers at the White Turkey. Wayne had some speed. So we tripped a little. And Wayne got it in his head that he wanted to test-drive the thing, to really open it up and see what it could do. We took it out to the old air base. Which is abandoned now except they keep some private planes out there.

We tried it out on the runway, but Wayne said it was too dark to enjoy. There were lights out there if we could find out how to cut them on.

Wayne took his pistol and shot the lock off of the power shack and cut the power and then started pulling switches. All these lights on the runways came on. And it was beautiful.

We jumped in the car and started out and really opened it up. We had it over 120 when that crazy airplane came down almost on top of us, landing.

That blew Wayne's mind.

As quick as he could he got it stopped and jumped out and ran for the woods. He probably thought it was somebody after him. He even took a couple of shots in the general direction of the plane.

I ran after him and we just ran on through the woods. We ran and ran, panting and sweating, until we came to a dirt road. We ran along it for a while, laughing now. There was a car, a station wagon belonging to Baptist College it turned out, parked there. Way out there all alone. We tiptoed and sneaked up to it. We peeped in.

In the very back, on a blanket, there was this couple, nobody we knew or had seen before, going at it like dogs in heat. They were sort of all fat and middle-aged. And ugly.

Wayne handed me his pistol. Then we went to the front. He pointed that the keys were there. We jumped in the front seat and he started it up and drove off down the road.

The folks in back sat up, bug-eyed and blinking. I pointed the gun at them.

"Don't stop on our account," Wayne told them. "We like company and we're planning a long ride."

"Where are you planning to take us?" the man said. He sounded drunk, thick-tongued.

"San Francisco," Wayne said. "You-all ever been there?"

The woman got hysterical. First she said how her husband would find out and then she just started crying and cussing and praying all at once. Wayne got bugged and told me to shoot her if she wouldn't shut up. But I wouldn't do that. So as soon as we hit the paved highway, he made them bail out of the back.

"What about my shoes?" the man said. "Let me find my freaking shoes at least."

But Wayne scratched out fast, just leaving them there by the side of the road.

I looked around and noticed we were headed southeast. Which is not the right direction if you plan to end up in San Francisco, California. But I didn't care. Just as long as we were moving, going *somewhere*.

"That was very rude about the shoes," I told Wayne.

"What about that old fart?" Wayne said. "Too cheap to rent a motel room."

ELEVEN

Signs of glory

Scissors flash bright keen click click
Hair falls heavy snip snip
Next he will shave my skull to be like his own bald
*   smooth cool clean*
Like a Catholic nun
Like the women the collaborators stripped naked then
*   shaved hairless*
Just so I am a nun and collaborator
Then
Then I will act
Then if ever
He is cutting off her hair just as she asked him to, and
she closes her eyes, feeling a great lightness and joy, know-
ing the time is here to act.

On her way to work, after another night of puzzling dreams, she saw the posters which had sprouted and bloomed in the night. Bright red, scarlet they were, and with large black letters.

OLD TIMEY TENT REVIVAL
SINGING AND PRAYING
PREACHING AND HEALING

The words blurred before her, but went on to announce additional entertainment by the child revivalist and his troupe: "Magic Tricks and Illusions/Secrets From the Ancient World/Bring the Whole Family." And at the bottom of the glaring poster was a photograph boldly labeled "The Fabulous Little David In Person." It was a boylike man in short pants with a loose shirt and a wide collar. He wore what, in its perfection, could only be a wig—long, curly, golden tresses. Beautiful false hair. Like a princess in a fairy tale. He had bright and staring eyes.

The boy-man possessed great powers. She could tell. She had powers, too, especially the powers of her dreams which were sent to her by God Almighty whether she liked it or not. She knew at once, swifter than thinking, when she stared into the eyes of the photograph, that this was to be a great testing of her, that the posters were to be taken as a sign. He, the boy-man, with his tricks and illusions, his memory of ancient secrets, his powers of healing, he could change everything here into new and strange things. And briefly that would be a blessing. Like a stage magician with his rabbits and doves, flashes and fires and puffs of colored smoke, he could dazzle an innocent congregation and lift them out of the weight of their suffering cages of skin and bones. For that moment they would feel lightened, uplifted, empty and contented. And then he would be gone. They would be left behind, soon to lose the vision of magic and gradually to rejoin their old company of ghosts, sorrows and secrets. Only *then*, don't you see?, they would be much poorer than ever, so much more the worse for wear. For now they would need visions. They would be starving with new hungers. And then the whole wonder of God's created world would fade and yellow like an old photograph. And then, having lost the beauty and the solace of the real world that God had made for them, would not they find all their natural sufferings compounded, ever after accompanied, like the background music in the movies, by the steady noise of lewd and demonic laughter?

She knew that the Creation was good. And this one great indisputable truth outweighed all other arguments and all evidence. Not only suffering in all its richness, its infinite variety of forms, but also all human acts and deeds, good and evil, were weighed in the balance, and, proving lighter than dust, were nothing. Nothing, therefore, was imperative. Nothing was commanded of her (yet) except that she cherish and preserve this truth. Having been so chosen, singled out, she must preserve herself for a great cause.

And it would be somehow within her power to change everything too. Not by deception. Not by the dazzle of dissatisfaction. But (when the signs came and the time was nigh) by doing something so startling and wonderful that the scales of their eyes would fall away and then, suddenly, old or young, rich or poor, lucky or losers, they would all be able to see Paradise Springs as it really is to be seen—not known or commonplace at all, but marvelous and stranger than China and Persia in old books, above all beautiful, world without end.

Even before she had finished staring into the eyes of the photograph on the poster, a boy on his way to school had broken her spell by stopping just long enough to draw a big handlebar mustache on the face of Little David. Only he was too late to spoil anything, for she had already been granted a flash of vision, a bright and enigmatic glimpse of her power and her duty.

All that remained now was to wait patiently for the sign. Meantime she could prepare for its coming, knowing it would surely come soon.

Her best friend, Darlene, who, for all her wild and thoughtless doings, could be taken almost as a living testament, a witness of the Truth, is as rich in health and body as earth itself. Darlene could go with her.

"He's just some kind of an overgrown midget," Darlene said. "But you know me. I'm game for anything once."

Alpha kept remembering the face in the photograph, trying to know it so well that, at any time, she could summon it up and see it all clearly and completely. A face at once wounded and cruel, hard and fixed like the face of a ventriloquist's dummy. Even in silence somehow speaking. Without words, without expression or gestures still saying, "I have seen the fires of hell and I know. I see hell now and always. I carry the fires of hell in me and with me. It is here and everywhere else. . . ."

Alpha knew all about hell from her dreams.

During that week she continued the usual pattern of her life, going to work at the bank, coming home again, her own face a blank mask too, mechanically and efficiently doing the things that had to be done. Not planning any action yet. Waiting patiently.

She wanted her parents' approval (as always like a child) for her going to the revival meeting.

Her father. He with a bum gimpy leg from the Korean War. He with a large fist forever shaking at stars and into the faces of the fools and knaves who overpopulate the world. He ridiculed the God which the knaves had invented to dupe the fools; first had invented, then killed, then dispossessed by sending Him off to live beyond blue sky, somewhere lonesome and far from Creation. Most of the time, except for trips to the post office (for his pension check, to mail his angry letters to newspapers and magazines and public figures), sitting grim as a scarecrow in a high-backed rocker on the front porch, quietly watching the knaves and fools hurrying to and fro in the inane, intricate pattern of their shabby dooms. Or else, from time to time, pint of whiskey beside him, at the big kitchen table, cleaning and caring for his arsenal of old rifles, pistols, and shotguns. Not grim then, but with a humming and whistling gaiety, preparing for the longed-for, inevitable day of reckoning when at last the U.N. and the Supreme Court would blithely and openly dare to raise and flaunt the red hammer and sickle flag of their true identity, and the Commie Commandos (a combined operations force composed of niggers, Jews, Catholics, and employees of the Internal Revenue Service) would march forth to take over the whole U.S.A. Which, he estimated and would say so whether anyone was listening or not, they would do easily, quickly, without meeting any real resistance from the idle and cowardly slobs, pointy heads, hippies and such. Except . . . Except for one small frame house in the town of Paradise Springs, Florida, a house with a shady patch of raggedy unkempt yard, a house needing a coat of paint, but containing one big *surprise for the bastards*. A house containing one old soldier, stiff leg and all, who would be heavily armed and waiting, able to make them earn his living space in blood.

Her mother . . . Who, maybe in spite of or maybe to spite him, keeps her lips zipped tight together in a pale thin scar, saying nothing (perhaps thinking nothing) about this subject. Goes alone once a week on Sunday to her own church, the Church of the Primitive Jesus, well beyond the edges of the town. Keeping its secrets and solace to herself. Otherwise spending her working hours hunched over her solid, old-fashioned Singer Sewing Machine, bent and squinting while the machine hums and buzzes and the needle leaps and dances, making fine clothes from patterns, of good materials and fit and at less than the price at the stores. Clothes for the children. Bridal gowns and widow's weeds. With the same skill and equal intensity making a dress for a confirmation or bright weeds for Darlene Blaze.

Her parents agreed that she and Darlene could go to the revival, as she wanted to, provided that Penrose went with them, to look after them. Penrose, keeping the sweet face of a choirboy, said he would be glad to go along to make sure the girls got there and back, safe and sound.

By Friday morning all that she needed was the final sign.

This time the sign came without full warning. Always before she had been prepared for the nature of the sign. First there would be nights of dreams, dreams riddled with things and beings which were terrifying, shameful to look upon. After a siege of nightmares, the angel would always appear in his brilliant uniform, his smile dazzling, his voice as soft and sweet as saxophones, to prepare her for the coming sign. Not that he could always be trusted. Sometimes he was the Devil in disguise. Sometimes, when she had been deceived and trusted blindly, there had been a sign which had caused her to do something bad or wrong. She had learned to be careful, through sorrow and bitter experience. But she accepted her sorrows humbly as a necessary chastisement. To be *chosen*, that truth lifted her spirit high and far, separated her true self forever from her dying body and its restless mind, dreaming or awake. Thus, even though body and mind could suffer, writhing upon a bed of nails, she could bear these things and smile because they were no more substantial than a shadow. She, her true and only self, was altogether elsewhere, free and alone in a garden of light and shade, sweet odors of flowers, coolness of breezes, and the fountains which tinkled continually with a lovely sound like the swaying of crystal chandeliers.

Silly little wisp of a shadow to weep and grind its teeth. She trained the shadow of herself like an animal. She trained her shadow to walk softly, to speak gently, and always to smile.

The sign came to her late Friday afternoon at the bank. They were closing for the weekend, and Alpha in her teller's cage was calmly checking and rechecking her records and receipts.

She was counting the envelope of cash which Mr. Pressy had brought in from his business. That was unusual, odd for him to come there himself. It was the first time she had seen or spoken to him in a long time, ever since she had gone with Darlene and stood naked under the hot lights of his studio to be photographed for money. She had done that, once and once only, to teach her body, that shadow, who was master and who was slave. She had forced her reluctant and virginal flesh to humiliate itself so that, ever after, it would be beyond humiliation. Of course, she told Darlene it was for the money. But she had put the money in the garbage, knowing that Penrose would find it there and find some mischievous use for it.

When he came into the bank, Mr. Pressy was, as always, very correct and polite, but as she accepted the envelope and his deposit slip, she felt her body burning behind the ears. Still not fully trained.

When she took up the handful of counted bills from the envelope, intending to stuff them into the large bag, which would be locked and placed in the vault until Monday, the green soiled bills came to life. They slithered and twisted in her grip. They hissed at her. And when, chills running the length of her backbone, she forced herself to look down at what she was holding, she saw it was a handful of poison snakes, green and terrible. She could have dropped them and run out of the bank screaming. Anyone else would have done so. She smiled inwardly, imagining how any one of the other girls would have run blindly out of the bank, into the wide and hectic arena of the shopping center parking lot, wild-eyed, all bathed in cold sweat, clawing at her clothing and crying out in an unknown tongue.

But Alpha would not do this; for she knew it for a test. She gritted her teeth and stared into the horrid nest of snakes, tightening her grip until her wrists ached and her hands trembled and her knuckles were dead white. And so she choked the life out of them. Dying at last, the snakes went limp and lapsed into their original form.

The other girls were already leaving. The manager

waited, anxious to lock everything up and go home. She had no time to interpret the sign. So, knowing only that whatever she must do concerned that money, she acted in good faith and scribbled the note to put in the locked bag: "I, Alpha Weatherby, owe the Peoples Bank, Fairview Center Branch, $543.77, which I am borrowing at this time, to do the work of the Lord." She dated and signed this note, put it in the bag, locked it and took it back to the vault, where the manager stood waiting.

He took it from her, smiled, and, as always, winking, mentioned something about the Friday night movies. That, too, was a test and a kind of humiliation for her. For she loved the movies, but he was a married man.

Once, long ago, when she had let herself flare at him out of pride and anger and vanity, he had said he was only "testing." So be it. He spoke more truly than he knew.

She hurried home and went into her room to meditate. Wide awake, she entered her secret garden, the place she had earned the right to enter. There she was as round and curved as a marble statue, in her new form, colored in ripeness and health like a peach. There she could wander free, in peace, like Eve herself, clad only in sunlight and soft breeze and the jeweled drops of the splashing fountains.

And there at last the angel came and joined her, brilliant in his military uniform, his high boots glistening like glass, the sword at his side glinting in the light. He took off his white leather gloves and took her hand in his. They walked together. Music played. There is no shame in that place.

After a time, she opened her eyes and got up from the

bed where she had been resting. She took her Bible from the bureau drawer. She kissed it and closed her eyes again. Keeping her eyes tight shut, she opened the Bible and placed it on her bureau. She jabbed with one finger into the open pages, held her fingertip where it touched, and opened her eyes to read the text chosen for her.

Where are now your prophets which prophesied unto you, saying the king of Babylon shall not come against you nor against this land?

She said the magic words to herself, out loud, several times, until, tasted and savored and swallowed, she had them by heart.

Then she allowed herself to look at her face in the mirror over the bureau. She stared into her own eyes and waited. Then she saw her reflected face begin to smile at her. A pretty girl, no matter if pale and thin, looked at her and smiled.

And she knew what must be done. It was a great sacrifice. No one would ever understand. Those who might love her would be deeply ashamed. All the rest would despise her. But she had been chosen, and, having been chosen, she had no choice of her own.

Calmly, joyously, she undressed herself completely and lay down again upon her bed. She closed her eyes. She could feel that her lips were still smiling, as she waited for the great gates of the garden to open and admit her, already listening for the first notes of the birdsong and the soft sound of the fountains and now, undeniably, the *clink-clink-clink* of the tall angel's spurs as he approached her.

She woke to her Darlene knocking on the door of her bedroom. She jumped up, slipped on her raincoat. She put the money in one pocket and her father's short-barreled .38-caliber revolver, called a "Banker's Special," into the other, and opened the door. Ready at last to go.

TWELVE

Checklist of the anonymous stranger
who flew the Twin Cessna

(a) Let's keep it short and sweet and to the point.

(b) If you think I'm going to give you my right name, you're crazy.

(c) Flying alone in own plane. Flight plan from Woodrum Field, Roanoke, Virginia, to Orlando, Florida.

(d) Destination: Disney World.

(e) Purpose of trip: Recreation. To meet wife and kids there.

(f) Trouble with oil pump north of Atlanta. Delay of several hours. Night flying necessary.

(g) Navigation not my bag. Navigated B-17 in W. W. II. Terrible navigator.

(h) Night navigation especially weak. Instruments on blink. Radio in bad shape.

(i) Was lost over north Florida somewhere. Looking for landing strip.

(j) Saw large fire near unidentified town. Circus tent on fire. Came down low to look at fire and search for landing strip.

(k) Suddenly many runway lights. Big field. Thought maybe somebody saw me.

(l) Couldn't raise anybody on radio. Got into landing pattern to come in.

(m) Touching down almost collided with white car coming wide open up middle of runway. Knees shaking.

(n) Field closed. Hanger, equipment shacks, some airplanes parked and tied down. No phone. Nothing . . .

(o) Car still sitting on runway, lights on.

(p) Taxied back to car. Car abandoned. Doors open, lights on. Nobody in sight.

(q) Borrowed fancy heap to drive to town and get oriented. Maybe get drink or two.

(r) Headed up highway in direction of glow of fire.

(s) Car pulled out of dark. Lights flashing. Pulled off of road.

(t) Got out. Said: "Boy am I glad to see you, Sheriff!"

(u) Huge monstro cop punches me and knocks me flat and groggy. Two others grab me. Take my pants.

(v) Crazy thing. They paint crotch and cock red, white, and blue. Then put bicycle lock (kid's trick) there.

(w) Big Sheriff: "You leave that girl alone, you hear?" They drive off.

(x) Plan: Get back in plane and go. Go anywhere.

(y) Problem: How to fly plane with bicycle lock on me?

(z) Tried to drive car back to field. Hard to drive with bicycle lock. Wrecked car in ditch.

(a-1) Nothing in glove compartment. Trunk contains

one (each) brown manila envelope and metal filing case, locked.

(a-2) Took stuff to field (one step at a time) to look at it in light.

(a-3) Couldn't open filing case. Brown envelope contained pictures and negatives etc. of naked girl.

(a-4) Can you beat that?

(a-5) Had to get lock off. Found file. Slow work.

(a-6) Found shack and cut off runway lights. Afraid somebody comes along and asks me to explain what's happened and what I'm doing.

(a-7) Finally able to get lock off. Dozed in plane.

(a-8) Dawn coming. Revved up engines and took off. Taking envelope and filing case with me.

(a-9) Climbing in circle, looking for landmark, anything. Circling over field and buildings of college or school campus.

(a-10) See lunatic, old fart in blanket, barefooted, come out of woods. Staggering in circles on campus. A wandering crazy bum.

(a-11) Buzzed bum several times, grass high. Ran him back and forth. Good runner when scared.

(a-12) Bum falls on knees, shakes fist at plane.

(a-13) Felt bad. Not *his* fault.

(a-14) Made one more pass. Bombed him with brown envelope.

(a-15) Envelope busts open. Pictures etc. blowing all over field.

(a-16) MAN IN PLANE BOMBS BUM WITH PICTURES OF NAKED GIRL.

(a-17) Make sense out of that.

(a-18) Pulling up I see bum chasing around field collecting pictures.

(a-19) Fly south.

(a-20) Drop filing case in middle of lake. Nice splash.

(a-21) Arrived safe in Orlando. Spent bundle at Disney World.

(a-22) Wife laughs at paint job. Believes nothing.

(a-23) Study map after fact. Draw big circle.

(a-24) *Never land a plane at Paradise Springs, Fla.!*

THIRTEEN

From a letter of Geneva Laseur
addressed to the Governor

I know you are a very busy person and have troubles of
your own. So I will try my best to be brief.

But I don't really know where to begin.

Well, one thing. I am sure that I got a fair trial and the
judge and the jury done what they thought was the right
thing to do.

I know that I have committed a crime and that I have
to be punished for it. But still I swear before God and man
alike that I was not guilty of conspiring with Billy Papp to
rob and kill the girl and Little David.

A lot came up at the trial that I didn't know anything
about. A whole lot of it was news to me. And there were
plenty of things to laugh at also. I do not blame the people
for laughing at me. I have been laughed at before. A huge
fat woman is usually a joke, any way you look at her.

When they laugh, I do not blame them because it is so hard not to laugh sometimes even when you don't want to.

I am used to it now.

I am at peace with myself and with God. And I do not mind their laughing any more. Laughter is God's gift to humankind. If it wasn't for that gift, we would most likely all be crying all the time.

That was the truth that Little David taught me and it truly changed my life.

One time I had been all healthy and good-looking. Many men thought I was beautiful and they desired me in that sense. Then I got this thing, this *condition*. The doctors couldn't agree on the name for it, but I surely got it, name or no name, and I just blew up in size like a big gas balloon.

Being a woman and even a beautiful one once, I was very hurt and confused. I cussed everything and everybody and most of all I hated myself.

More than one time I tried to kill myself. But I was always too scared of the pain to do a good job of it.

I was a lost soul.

Then one time I went to a revival where they claimed to have healing. Because I would try anything. When I kneeled down, Little David put his hands on my head. And he whispered to me that there was no way he could make me young and thin and beautiful again, but he could *heal* me nevertheless.

I was very mistrustful and suspicious. But I went to him again later, privately, and he talked me into joining up with him and his group. The way it worked with me was very slow and gradual. I saw all kinds of suffering and tribulation all the time. And I saw how he suffered too, and always had, being so little and sickly and all. And after a

266

while I came to realize that I did not care all that much about myself any more. Not enough to hate myself. Little by little, I stopped worrying about me, myself, and I all the time.

And that is how I came to love him. I stopped hating me and started loving him. And he loved me, too. And then it was a true glory, for I was truly healed.

We became common-law man and wife together and we shared one bed. I know that people would not want to believe this, and even if they did it would just make them laugh to imagine the two of us together. That is because they could not fully understand. I have been, as my record plainly proves, a prostitute and a hard-living woman in my time. I know all about sex and what can be done. And I know from experience that love and sex are not exactly the same thing. I had plenty of experience both good and bad.

Nobody has a right to know what went on between us privately. All I can say without being ashamed is that I loved him and he loved me and it was glory. There were times when I felt as light and frail as a little girl again and when he was a giant as big as a mountain.

Now I want to explain how things happened that night. I have seen and known many crazy things in my lifetime. And many times I have had to wonder if I wasn't crazy myself. But I have never seen anything to beat that night.

It is true that I did notice that young woman, the late Alpha Weatherby, because when I was first passing the collection plate, she reached in her pocket and produced a big fistful of bills and just plunked it in the plate, *deposited* it so to speak, like maybe an old candy wrapper or something.

A thing like that would be enough to make anybody take notice. And she and her friend had an argument about her giving away all that money. Her friend wanted to snatch it back, but Miss Alpha Weatherby wouldn't let her.

Naturally I pointed her out to Little David as soon as I had a chance.

Later on in the service she came up front to witness and to be saved. And her friend wasn't with her. She put another wad of cash in my plate up there. Then she spoke to me and asked me if she could see David in private later.

She did not seem crazy. She was very soft-spoken and she looked sincere to me at the time. And anyway she had already put so much money in the plate that I couldn't just refuse her.

I told her that since the last part of the service would soon be over, why didn't she come with me now and I would show her the trailer where she could wait to see him and be comfortable.

That seemed to suit her, so I took her out the back of the tent and over to our trailer.

I better admit to something since it can't do any harm anyway now. That wasn't the first time I ever took a woman to our trailer like that. In our line of work we depend a good deal on people who get moved by the spirit and end up giving away a lot of cash as an offering. We never went out of our way to discourage them. That may have been wrong in a way, but we had to keep alive and keep going. And then, naturally, Little David had a way of attracting various kinds of women to him and his cause. Some of these women could be weird. So I would keep my eyes open and be available in case anything went wrong.

If I had ever suspected that Alpha Weatherby was crazy

I would never have led her to our trailer in a million years. But she appeared to be a sincere and deeply religious person and I guess that fooled me.

We went inside the trailer and I turned on all the lights and started the air conditioning to make it comfortable. While I was doing that she emptied her pockets on the bunk. I saw the pile of money and I also saw the pistol. And I knew then that there was trouble. But I didn't want to let on that I had noticed anything strange.

"Are you comfortable?" I said to her. "The air conditioning will have it nice and cool in a few minutes."

"I'm fine," she said. "But I think I'll just slip out of this raincoat if you don't mind."

And I said to myself, Geneva, this is a crazy world and maybe you are crazy, too, from living in it. But this girl takes the all-time prize and you better get your ass in gear and warn David what is waiting for him in the trailer.

I excused myself politely and started back to tell David.

Only by that time the snakes had got loose in the tent and then the tent was catching fire.

In the confusion I couldn't even find him.

Everything was all going on at the same time. It is a wonder I just didn't keel over dead with a stroke. I tried to catch my breath and think. I remembered that Billy Papp owned a pistol. I thought I had better go borrow it quick before that girl had a chance to do anything with hers.

When I came busting into Papp's trailer, there was her friend, the other one, dancing around. I tell you, I thought the end of the world was upon us. But I got Papp's gun and I remember *running* back to our trailer. I hardly ever run if I can help it because it is so hard on my heart. But at that time I didn't even think of that. I just started running. People were all milling around and I had to push and shove my way through them. I guess it did look wild, a great big fat woman, waving a pistol in her hand, and trying to run. It was not a sight you would forget right away. I wasn't surprised when they testified about how I looked and acted.

When I got inside the trailer everything stopped dead. It looked like a movie or a photograph instead of something real. There she was with all of her hair cut off, standing with the hair all around her bare feet. She had David's straight razor in her hand, testing the sharpness of it with her thumb.

I knew she was going to kill him. I knew that she was going to kill him and cut off his head. I could tell it all in her eyes. And I could tell that he did not know it, either.

I did the only thing I could do. I started shooting with the pistol. I did not intend to hit anyone. I was not aiming at anybody. Just shooting to stop everything from happening.

I must have accidentally hit him first because he fell over by the bunk. Then she came toward me with the razor. And so I didn't see him grab her pistol. I was now pointing my pistol at her, in self-defense, and pulling the trigger. But it was not stopping her, and I realized that my pistol was empty and just going *click, click, click*. Then there was the loud noise again only it was her pistol this time, and she fell flat right in front of me. I saw her eyes go blank and dead as she fell. And I saw his eyes fading too as he fell off the bunk.

Papp came into the trailer and snatched his pistol back from me.

Right behind him came the police.

It all happened real fast and just the way I told it. And nobody had said a word to each other. The first ones to say anything were the police.

I still do not understand some parts of it. I know I was not trying to shoot David. That was an accident. But something else I am pretty sure of now. It was also an accident when David shot the girl. He intended to hit me, but his aim wasn't steady and she stepped right into the line of fire. What he must have thought was that I was out of my mind, going berserk out of jealousy. I know that's what he must have thought. And if he thought that, then he thought I had shot him on purpose.

I am sorry I never had a chance to explain to him.

I am sorry he is dead and I am sorry for the girl too.

And I am sorry for Billy Papp. Because he didn't really have anything to do with it. Knowing him as well as I do, I expect he probably was going to steal our money and take off. But, then, there is no proof that we ever collected all that money anyway. There is only what was left of the girl's money in the trailer.

Your Honor, I know I am guilty. But I am not guilty of the whole thing that they said. It is not true that me and Billy conspired together with David to kill that girl. All I can say is I know how it was because I was there.

But I have no real complaints against anyone.

I have to ask your mercy because I am afraid of jail and I don't want to die in there.

If you can find some way to let me off, I will be grateful with all my heart.

But if you cannot find a reason or a way, I won't blame you.

If I have to stay in jail, I will surely die there. I cannot promise to be brave about all this, but I will do the best I can. For I believe that Almighty God, who has always loved me, will be kind to me in my misery. And one day I will shed my weary flesh and bones like old clothes and then my heart will be light again. I will be so light I can float on the air.

I am sorry about all the trouble I have caused you and the state of Florida.

There is only one more trouble I want to cause anybody. I have a married sister in Fort Worth, Texas. She is happily married to a chiropractor there. She feels bad and guilty about me because I put her through school and everything but she was always ashamed of me. She has never done anything for me or had a chance to. When I die I hope you will send my body to her so she can see that it gets buried properly. That will give her a chance to make up for what she hasn't done and to feel better about herself.

Don't we all need a chance for something like that?

Yours truly,
Geneva Laseur